DOG WHISPERER

STORM WARNING

DOG WHISPERER

STORM WARNING

By Nicholas Edwards

NEW YORK

An Imprint of Macmillan

 Printed in the United States of America by R. R. Donnelley & Sons Company, Harrisonburg, Virginia. For information, address Square Fish, 175 Fifth Avenue, New York, NY 10010.

Library of Congress Cataloging-in-Publication Data Available

ISBN 978-0-312-37095-4

Book designed by Barbara Grzeslo
Square Fish logo designed by Filomena Tuosto

First Edition: December 2011

mackids.com

3 5 7 9 10 8 6 4 2

AR: 6.0 / LEXILE: 970L

DOG WHISPERER

STORM WARNING

1

Zachary wouldn't pose properly—and, in Emily's opinion, the fact that he was a dog was not a good enough excuse. She had been trying to draw a portrait of him ever since she'd gotten home from school, but all she had managed to do so far was a few wasted pages with the beginnings of pictures, none of which looked right *at all*. So she just kept flipping to the next page in her sketchbook and trying again—and again, and *again*.

It was September, and the sky was that perfect bright blue shade, with almost no clouds, and a clean backdrop of tall green fir trees across the sound. The ocean was an even darker, clear blue, with the water just choppy enough to look interesting. So her plan had been for Zachary to sit sweetly on their dock, while she did her best to capture him looking dignified and noble.

Zachary's plan seemed to be to sit still for about thirty seconds, and then race along the rocky shoreline to bark at seagulls, crawl under bushes to find one of his many battered tennis balls, roll around in the grass, and gallop up to the back deck every so often to drink heartily from his water dish.

Then, he would run over to her, wagging his tail. He kept trying to climb on her lap, even though—since he was a really *big* dog, over a hundred pounds—he weighed more than she did. Once, he even grabbed her pencil out of her hand and cocked his head, to indicate that he wanted her to throw it for him.

"Zack," she said patiently, and turned to yet another clean page on her pad. "I only want to draw you for, like, *five* minutes. I just need to get a really good outline down, and then we can play and I'll finish it later."

Zachary's ears perked up when he heard the word "play," and he barked once.

Okay. Maybe she should give up and spend the rest of the afternoon throwing things for him to fetch, and they could go for a nice, long walk down their dirt road. But, seriously, all she wanted to do was sketch the bare outlines, and maybe capture his expression. Zack always had a good expression. He looked really *smart*. He was a white retriever mix, which meant that she had to do a lot of shading on the paper to make him stand out from the background—which was why she had to *practice* a lot.

"Could we try one more time?" she asked him

Zachary tilted his head curiously, and she slipped her hand under his collar—a very flattering red plaid pattern—and led him down to the dock again.

"If you could just sit for a couple of minutes, I promise I'll draw really, really fast," she said.

He wagged his tail and sat down on the weathered wood.

"That's great!" she said, and hurried back to her sketch pad and started sketching as quickly as she could.

She would worry about the colors later, but what she really wanted to do was re-create the alert, kind light in his brown eyes. Her parents had started signing her up for art classes when she was about five years old, so she had learned a lot—but she kind of knew just enough to realize how much she *didn't* know. And the art teacher at her new junior high school in Brunswick was a *real* artist, who had recently moved up to Maine from Provincetown, and Emily was hoping that he would be able to help her learn lots of advanced drawing techniques. Mr. Reed had even said that he might start an after-school oil painting class soon, if enough students were interested!

Zachary was being very good and patient now, and she sketched and shaded swiftly. He was sort of slouching, though, and she wished that he would sit up straighter, and maybe even lift a paw for her, like Lassie always did in the television reruns she had seen.

"Could you please hold your paw up?" she asked, and demonstrated with her left hand. "Like this?"

Zack looked distinctly puzzled.

Sometimes, she thought he understood every word she said, so she talked to him a lot, but they actually communicated *more* than that. It was sort of—psychic. Which was really cool, but also kind of unnerving. They had the exact same dreams and nightmares pretty often, and there were other times when she would find herself thinking something and then realize that, no, *Zachary* was thinking it. Food was usually a big clue since she, for example, had never wanted to run over to their neighbors' backyard and grab a steak off the grill and race into the woods to eat the whole thing by herself. She didn't go around telling people about it, because she wasn't sure what it all meant, but—well—the simple truth was that she was almost *sure* that she and Zack could read each other's minds. And she mostly liked the idea, except when it made her a little bit nervous. Her friends, Bobby and Karen, were the only two who really knew about it, and they had both just said, "Wow. Cool!"

She closed her eyes and concentrated on an image of Zack sitting on their dock, with his right paw up in the air, looking smart and confident and *totally* Hollywood. Then, she opened her eyes to see Zachary shifting uncomfortably on the wooden planks. He raised his right paw for a couple of seconds, then made a small sound and lowered it, panting slightly.

"I'm sorry," she said, feeling very guilty. When she had found him washed up on the rocks in front of their house about six weeks earlier, he had been a lost, injured stray, and among other things, his left foreleg had been broken. He had just gotten his cast off a few days ago, but his leg must still be bothering him. "That was really stupid of me."

She closed her eyes again and pictured him lifting his *left* paw instead, so that most of his weight would be on his stronger right leg. Zack thumped his tail on the dock and held up his left paw this time.

"Oh, great, that's perfect," she said, focusing intently on her drawing. "You're a very good dog."

Zachary wagged his tail again and sat in that exact position—for about another minute. Then, a squirrel chirped in a nearby tree, and Zack instantly dashed over there, barking playfully.

She dropped her pencil and pad, and lay down in the grass. A few clouds were starting to roll in, along with a tiny bit of fog, and the air smelled of salt. But mostly, it was perfectly bright and clear, and beginning to feel like fall.

"It looked like you had him for a few minutes there," her father said, startling her a little, since she hadn't heard him come out to the backyard.

"More like a few *seconds*," Emily said, and lifted herself onto one elbow to see that Zack was now over by their kind of bedraggled garden, digging a hole. "Mom's not going to like that."

Her father glanced in that direction. "Well, maybe he'll get some of the weeds." Then, he paused. "Are we supposed to yell, 'No, no! Bad dog! No!'?"

Emily grinned. Her father had grown up in New York City and had never had pets—until she got a kitten when she was six, who was named Josephine. He had adjusted to having a small, cranky cat, but as far as she could tell, he still couldn't quite get used to the idea of them living with a really big *dog*.

"No, Zack!" her father said experimentally.

Zack kept digging.

"He seems not to recognize my authority," her father said.

Well—yeah. Emily just grinned.

Her father motioned towards the grass. "Is that comfortable?"

There was a small rock digging into the back of her hip, but other than that, the grass was nice and thick and warm, so Emily nodded.

Her father was wearing nice khakis and a grey sweater with a white oxford shirt underneath. Emily thought of them as his "professor clothes," even though he usually dressed that way even when the college *wasn't* in session. He looked down at the ground without much enthusiasm, but then sat down—cautiously—on the grass.

"Do your students recognize your authority?" she asked curiously.

Her father thought about that. "The freshmen do. The seniors, less so."

Sometimes, her parents invited some of their students over for little parties and potluck suppers and so forth. Emily usually felt shy and stayed upstairs for most of the time, but she had noticed that the freshmen *also* always seemed shy, while the older students and teaching assistants were much more sure of themselves.

Her father stretched out on the grass, somewhat clumsily, folding his hands behind his head.

"So," he said after a few minutes. "What are you doing?"

"Looking at the sky," Emily said. "What are *you* doing?"

Her father sighed. "I don't know. Just lying here, wondering where it all went wrong."

Which was alarming, and Emily stared at him.

"Kidding," he said.

Oh. She relaxed and settled back down.

They lay there, staring at the sky and the thickening clouds and the light fog moving across the channel from the open sea. Digging in the garden must have gotten boring, because Zachary came over and flopped down next to them. Instead of watching the sky, though, he just fell asleep.

"I hope we don't get Lyme disease," her father said after a while.

Emily laughed—although now that he had mentioned it, she kind of hoped so, too.

It was very peaceful, resting there, and Emily considered taking a little nap herself.

"Were the three of you struck by a particularly efficient gust of wind?" Emily's mother asked from somewhere behind them.

Emily laughed, her father said, "Yes," and Zack thumped his tail twice. Other than that, they all stayed where they were, lying in the grass.

"Are any of you going to get up?" Emily's mother asked.

"Well, I don't know," Emily's father said. "It's very pleasant down here."

"Except for the Lyme disease," Emily said.

"That's my least favorite part," her father agreed.

"Well, okay," her mother said. "I guess I'll eat all of this Thai takeout by myself."

Zack scrambled to his feet, and Emily and her father immediately sat up.

The food smelled great, and Emily realized that she was completely starving. She'd had some peach yoghurt when she got home from school, but apparently that hadn't come even close to spoiling her appetite.

The weather was so nice that her parents decided that they should eat at the picnic table on the deck. Emily carried plates, napkins, and silverware outside, while her mother set out the plastic containers of food with a bunch of serving spoons, and her father poured a glass of milk for Emily and iced tea for him and her mother.

Emily had been a vegetarian since she was nine, and her parents were always worried that she wasn't getting enough nutrition. But since she was *already* an inch taller than her mother—even though she wasn't going to turn twelve for another nine days—she figured that she was probably getting enough to eat.

On the other hand, since she was adopted, for all she knew she was just *naturally* tall, and it had nothing to do with whether she got enough protein at every meal. Her grandparents worried about it even more than her parents did, and her grandmother on her father's side was always saying things like, "How about just *one* piece of brisket? That would be okay, right?"

Her parents were sharing a chicken satay appetizer, and Emily was eating a steamed vegetable dumpling, when she suddenly started thinking about cars. Which was totally weird because she really wasn't at all *interested* in cars.

No, not *cars*. Car. Just one. She closed her eyes,

trying to concentrate. Was the car in the air? It seemed as though—

"Emily, are you all right?" her mother asked.

She opened her eyes. "What?" She shook her head, feeling a little disoriented. "I mean, yeah."

Her mother reached over to feel her forehead with the back of her hand, to see if she had a fever or something. "Well, you look awfully tired. Do you have much homework?"

Emily shook her head. "Not really." So far, seventh grade was *really* different from sixth grade, but they still weren't getting a lot of homework yet. "Just some vocabulary, and—"

The image of the car came back vividly into her mind, but this time it seemed to be falling? And there was a person. Was someone trapped *under* a car?

Zack was standing by her side, looking up at her urgently. Then, once he was sure she had gotten the message, he turned and dashed out of the yard.

Okay, she didn't need any more hints that there was some kind of an emergency. Emily dropped her fork on the table and ran after him as fast as she could.

She didn't know where, or why, or how—but somewhere nearby, she was *sure* that there was a person trapped underneath a car!

2

When they got to the end of the driveway, Zack didn't hesitate at all, veering to his right and galloping down the road. Emily did her best to keep up with him, but he outpaced her with a fast, efficient lope.

Up ahead of them, there was a car parked by the side of the dirt road. One side was propped up, as though it had a flat tire, and she could see a man's legs sticking out from underneath. It was Dr. Henrik's car. He was a retired professor from the college, who lived a few houses away from them.

She slowed down, since a flat tire didn't exactly seem like a big deal. Sometimes, Zack overreacted, or misinterpreted a little. He had once gotten very panicky when her cat, Josephine, started playing around in the crawl space in their attic—except that she had done it lots of times before, and seemed to think it was funny to hide in the narrow wooden spaces.

"Zack, it's okay!" she said after him. "Come on back!"

But then, she heard a faint yell and realized that Dr. Henrik was calling for help.

She also realized that the car was sagging badly to one side. The jack seemed to be buckling, and the car was going to come down right on top of him!

Emily started running again. "Mom! Dad! Call 911!" she yelled over her shoulder.

"Help," a muffled voice said. "I'm trapped!"

If they didn't hurry, the car was going to collapse completely, and crush him!

They had to *do* something, but she wasn't sure what, exactly. Emily had read that sometimes, in emergencies, people had superhuman strength and actually *could* lift cars off people, but—well, it looked really heavy.

She looked at Zack for a second, wondering if he felt indecisive, too. But, as far as she could tell, he didn't because he was already digging frantically at the dirt with his front paws.

That made sense, because maybe Dr. Henrik could squeeze out from underneath the car that way—except, no, Zachary was too close to the jack, and if it slid down into the hole, the car would fall on top of both of them!

"No, Zack, over *here*," she said, and used her hands to dig on the other side of Dr. Henrik, away from the front end of the car.

Zack bounded over next to her and began digging again.

"Please," Dr. Henrik gasped. "Go get help!"

It didn't seem like there was *time* to go get help. "Mom! Dad!" she yelled, using a flat rock to try and dig faster. "We're over here!"

They had cleared out a small trough, and Zack grabbed Dr. Henrik's pants leg in his teeth and pulled forcefully. Realizing what Zack was trying to do, Emily grabbed Dr. Henrik's other ankle, trying to pull him into the shallow hole they'd dug—just as the front end of the car began to creak and sway—and then sagged down another six inches or so.

Okay, the problem was that they could drag his legs, but the rest of him was still stuck. They maybe had to dig the hole partway under the car, too. Zack was way too big to fit, but *she* could squeeze under there. So she crawled carefully underneath the car, trying not to jar anything, and used the flat rock to try and dig.

"Emily, get out, it isn't safe down here," Dr. Henrik said weakly. "Please, go find your parents."

"I'm going to dig right here," Emily said, already doing it. "So we can get you out."

"*No*," he said, his voice rasping. "It's too dangerous."

Emily figured they really didn't have time to argue about it, especially since the car was shifting ominously above her; the back tires sinking deeper into the sandy dirt. She dug as fast as she could, but didn't seem to be making much progress. Luckily, she could hear footsteps pounding on the road, so she would have help very soon.

"Emily, get out from there!" her mother shouted.

"He's trapped," Emily shouted back, out of breath from the effort of digging. "The jack's, like, *bending*."

"Come out from there *right this instant*," her mother said in a very, very fierce voice.

Emily hesitated, since she had never heard her mother sound quite that serious before. "I'll be right back," she said to Dr. Henrik, and crawled backwards, until she was out on the road again.

"Here," her mother said abruptly and pushed a cell phone into her hand. "Stand back there, out of the way, and call 911."

Emily quickly dialed the numbers and reported the emergency and their location. The dispatcher promised to send the police and fire department right away.

In the meantime, her parents and Zack were all digging and pulling, and it looked as though their neighbor was almost free. But, for some reason, they *still* couldn't get him out.

"I'm sorry, it's caught," Dr. Henrik said, sounding very frustrated—and maybe kind of scared, too. "I can't get loose."

Emily peered under the car, and saw that his shirt was snagged in the car's undercarriage and that he couldn't reach it. Before anyone had time to tell her she *couldn't*, she squirmed back in there, trying to ignore the sounds of metal creaking and the sense that the car was swaying back and forth above them.

"I see it!" she said, and grabbed at the cloth with both hands until she heard it tear.

And just like that, Dr. Henrik was loose, and was being pulled free by her parents; and she was alone under the car, which seemed to be sinking lower with every passing second.

"Emily, crawl out!" her mother shouted. "I can't reach you!"

For a second, Emily wanted to panic, but she felt something grabbing her jeans leg. A hand? No, it was *teeth*. Zack was tugging on her jeans leg.

As he started to drag her out, she felt her parents' hands fasten around her other ankle—and she was yanked out to safety just as the jack finally collapsed, and the car came smashing down to the ground with a huge crashing sound!

It was so quiet for a few seconds that the sound seemed to echo, and Emily blinked, then looked around to make sure that everyone was okay. Dr. Henrik was sitting up on the road, seeming a little dazed and holding his side like he had maybe hurt his ribs. Her parents were checking her over, looking completely frantic, and Zack was pacing back and forth, whining anxiously.

"Are you all right?" her mother asked. "Are you *hurt*?"

Emily shook her head. "No, I'm fine." She was maybe a little *surprised*, because everything had happened so quickly, but that was it.

She could hear sirens and see flashing lights, as the police, and an extra squad car, turned onto their road. Then, the local ambulance corps showed up, along with the fire department—and a reporter and photographer from the *Bailey's Cove Courier*.

It was all kind of noisy and hectic, as the paramedics bundled Dr. Henrik onto a gurney, so they could take him to the hospital in Brunswick and make sure he was okay. One of the police officers went down to Dr. Henrik's house to get his wife, who had been working inside on her computer, and was now quite upset because she had had no idea that so much drama had been taking place only about a quarter of a mile away.

The paramedics also checked Emily over, although the only problem she had found was that there was a bunch of axle grease on her jeans and her brand-new purple t-shirt. Which was too bad because she really *liked* the shirt, and probably wasn't going to be able to wear it again, except maybe for things like raking leaves and weeding the garden.

The police asked a few questions and took their statements, and the reporter *wanted* to ask questions, but her parents politely declined to be interviewed. The photographer took a couple of pictures of Zack, though.

When they finally walked back home, her parents were *so* quiet that it made Emily nervous.

"You must never do *anything* like that again," her father said.

"*Ever*," her mother agreed. "You could have been

very seriously hurt, or— You *have* to be more careful, Emily."

Now that she thought about it, the whole thing *had* been pretty scary. "I know, I really wasn't thinking," Emily said. "I'm sorry."

"Well, you were very brave," her father said. "But it was an extremely dangerous thing to do."

After she had promised never to do it again, and her parents both hugged her—and then hugged Zack—Emily was pretty sure they all felt a lot better. And the good news was that Dr. Henrik was okay! Mrs. Henrik had called and told them that he had broken a couple of ribs, and was being kept in the hospital overnight for observation, but that he would be just fine.

The sun had gone down, and all of their food had gotten cold, so they ended up carrying everything into the kitchen and heating their supper up in the microwave.

Josephine came downstairs and perched up on the counter, where she could watch all of them with great disapproval. She was a very small tiger cat, with a white patch on her chest, and rather sly yellow eyes. She and Zachary weren't exactly the best of friends, but they were reasonably comfortable with each other, and at night, they both always slept on Emily's bed.

"So, wait a minute. How did you know Dr. Henrik was in trouble?" her father asked, out of nowhere.

Emily still hadn't figured out a way to tell her parents that she kind of, maybe, *totally* could read her dog's mind—without sounding like a nut.

"Um, you didn't hear him?" she asked. "Calling for help?"

Her parents shook their heads.

Oh. She felt shy about telling them the whole truth, but she didn't want to lie, either. So she wasn't sure how to answer. "It was mostly just Zack," she said. "I followed him when he ran. I guess he knew that something was wrong."

"Well, he's a smart dog," her mother said, and patted him.

Zachary wagged his tail, but never took his eyes off the remaining skewer of chicken satay.

"Can he have it?" Emily asked.

Her mother shrugged. "Sure, why not?"

When Emily started to feed it to him, Josephine meowed in protest, and Emily got up to feed some of the chicken to her, too. It was clear at once that her cat didn't care for the spices, but Josephine stubbornly ate her entire share, anyway.

Zack didn't even seem to *notice* that the chicken was spicy, since he gulped it down so quickly.

After supper, Emily went upstairs to get cleaned up. Her mother was going to try and soak her shirt and jeans in detergent, to see if she could get the stains out. There was, like, motor oil and axle grease and just plain old dirt, and she had to take a really long bath and wash her hair three times before she was clean. And even then, she still felt kind of sandy.

Her mother always worried a lot about her hair because it tended to be coarse and dry, and she would buy her all kinds of special leave-in conditioners. It always made Emily laugh when she saw her very blond mother curled up on the couch reading books about African-American hair care.

When her mother's friend, Dr. Jacobs, who was also African-American, came over, she was always full of "yes, shea butter is good, but pomegranate oil is really better" beauty tips. Her mother would nod a lot and look sheepish during these sessions, although the truth was, she wasn't that good at fixing her *own* very straight and unchallenging hair, so Emily had decided to cut her some serious slack on the whole issue.

Once, when they were visiting her grandparents in New York, her mother had even taken her on the subway up to Harlem, to a special hair-braiding place, where everyone else in the styling room seemed to be both bemused—and somewhat resigned—to see them there. Or, at any rate, to see her mother there. The whole process had taken *hours*, and Emily had ended up not liking how she looked; and the beads were always clacking whenever she moved her head, which was really annoying. She wore the braids for a few weeks, until she convinced her mother to let her have them cut off—and she had never gotten it done again. A ponytail was about as ambitious as she got with her hair these days.

After she had changed into her nightgown, she studied her vocabulary, did some algebra equations, and then answered email and sent instant messages to her friends and one of her cousins in California until it was time to go to bed.

Her father took Zachary out for his last walk of the night and then brought him back upstairs to her room.

Her mother had already come in to say good night to her, and Emily was under the covers, trying to stay awake.

Zachary enthusiastically greeted Josephine, who was sitting on the rug—and she hissed at him. Undaunted, Zachary went over to drink some water from his dish in the corner and then bounded up onto the bed, his tail wagging happily.

"Hi, Zack," Emily said, patting him on the head. "Thanks for taking him out, Dad."

"No problem." Her father sat down on the edge of the bed, so that he could give her a hug good night. Then, he looked at her with a serious expression. "Your mother and I were very proud of what you did tonight."

Emily was surprised that hearing him say that made her feel self-conscious. It wasn't as though she had thought at all about what she was doing; she had just been trying to help, if she could.

"But, never again," he said.

"*Never*," she promised.

And she definitely hoped Zachary was reading her mind, and agreed with that!

3

When Emily woke up the next morning, her first thought was that she was *really* glad that it was Friday, and her second thought was that her birthday was now only eight days away!

She could smell eggs cooking downstairs—and bacon, yuck—but her mother would probably cook some soy bacon for her, if she wanted some. She wasn't crazy about the texture, but eggs were kind of boring by themselves.

It turned out that her mother was making her a cheese and vegetable omelet, along with some toast and applesauce. Emily was pretty hungry, but she shared some of her breakfast with Zack and Josephine—who both seemed pleased by this, although entirely uninterested in the onions and mushrooms.

Sometimes, whichever one of her parents had an earlier class to teach that day would drive her to school, but usually, she would go up to the end of the dirt road and wait for the bus. Today was a take-the-bus day. Her friend Bobby was supposed to catch the bus *with* her, but he nearly always overslept; and she would end up sitting shyly in a seat by herself, with lots of eighth and ninth graders she didn't know. When she was alone, no one ever said much of anything to her—good or bad—but it always felt as though they were trying too hard *not* to notice that she was the only person of color on the bus. Maybe it was her imagination, but it really did feel that way.

One time, an eighth grader—who she knew was just trying to be nice—asked if she was going to try out for the basketball team, and probably had no idea why she said *no* so very stiffly.

It *might* just have been because, yeah, okay, she was tall for her age, but Emily didn't think so. Anyway, she just shook her head, and said, "No, I don't really like basketball." The eighth-grade girl looked surprised, and said, "Oh," and that was the end of that.

The bus stop was right by Cyril's Mini-Mart, which was a tiny but unusually well-stocked little store, where all of the locals bought milk and newspapers and fish hooks and lightbulbs, and whatever else they needed on a given day. Cyril was *ancient*, but always full of energy and loud opinions. Bobby had once tried to shoplift a candy bar from the Mini-Mart when he was about four years old—and Cyril had never forgiven him, or allowed him to set foot inside, ever since. Cyril also disliked tourists, but since they gave him lots of business, he would grudgingly allow them to shop to their heart's content.

There was a faded white picnic table, with two benches, in front of the store, and there was *always* at least one person sitting there, drinking coffee. But, most of the time, there would be a small group of locals, chatting about nothing much and trading very exaggerated stories for hours on end. Tourists *loved* the sight of "real Mainers" talking, and almost always stopped to take pictures of them. During the height of the season, some of the regulars would dress in the most stereotypical Maine outfits they could find, and play up the whole crusty-New-Englander thing in a big way.

But now, the summer was over, so people were back to wearing their normal crewneck sweaters and jeans and Top-Siders, and Red Sox and New England Patriots gear. The overalls and torn flannel shirts and battered hats full of fishing lures and so forth had gone back into storage until next summer, for the most part.

This particular morning, Mr. Washburn, Mr. Bolduc, and Mrs. Parsons were all sitting at the table. Mr. Washburn was a retired Harvard professor, Mr. Bolduc and his wife operated a small Christmas tree farm, and Mrs. Parsons was a poet. Emily decided to go keep them company while she was waiting, since they were almost certainly swapping tales, the way they did pretty much *every* day, lounging in that exact same spot. She always liked listening to the conversations, even when she'd heard the stories before. Besides, there were *always* new and interesting details added every time the stories got told.

They all waved at her, and she waved back.

"Mrs. Henrik was by here a little while ago," Mr. Washburn said, "telling us all about it. Good show!"

Emily shrugged shyly. "It was all Zack. We just followed him."

"Still, good show to *all* of you," Mr. Washburn said.

As she started to walk over to the table, she heard a loud rustling in the underbrush behind her. She paused, wondering if Zack could have gotten out and followed her, or if it might be a wild animal, when someone said, "*Pssst!*"

She peered through the tall grass and branches—and saw Bobby crouching near a wild blueberry bush.

"What are you doing?" she asked.

"Hiding," he said.

Okay, she could have figured out that one on her own.

"Why?" she asked.

"Cyril," he said. "Why else?" He stepped cautiously out of the bushes, wearing jeans, Nike high-tops, and a Boston Bruins hoodie. At their new school, he had managed to talk almost everyone into calling him "Bob," but she had known him since they were little and she couldn't think of him as anything other than "Bobby." "Zack didn't follow you down here?" he asked.

Emily glanced around, just in case. "Not yet." Zachary was remarkably clever about finding ways to sneak outside, even when they thought he had been safely closed up for the day.

Bobby shook his hair out of his eyes—he had kind of a long-haired-surfer thing going these days, even though he never did anything more than ride on a Boogie board a little—and glanced around to make sure Cyril was nowhere in sight.

"You study for the vocabulary test?" he asked.

Emily nodded. "Did you?"

"Nope," Bobby said cheerfully.

Which was the answer she would have predicted. "It was really easy," Emily said. "If you looked at the list right now, you'd get an A."

He shrugged. "No big deal. I *never* get an A."

That was true, but Emily was sure it was because he didn't try, not because he couldn't do it.

Just then, Cyril came lumbering out of the store, carrying a plastic bag of trash, which he packed into the small Dumpster by the side of the building.

"Good morning, Emily!" he said brightly, and then pointed a stern finger at Bobby. "You're not to stand on my property, young punk."

Bobby looked down at his feet. "Where's the line, sir?"

Cyril grumbled, but came over and dragged his boot heel through the dirt to make a distinct boundary. He always wore old, but well-shined, army boots, which Emily had assumed were the ones he had used when he was serving in Vietnam. But he had once told her father that he was actually on his fifth pair since then.

"Not one inch over that," Cyril said, once he had completed the line.

Bobby nodded, and moved so that the tips of his sneakers were precisely behind it.

Cyril narrowed his eyes. "Are you being smart there, you ne'er-do-well?"

Bobby shook his head. "No, sir. Smart is too hard for me."

Cyril frowned harder, stroking his big white mustache thoughtfully. "I don't know. That sure sounds like smart mouth to me."

Emily decided to jump in. "Sir, is it true that the Black Bears recruited a really good goalie this year?"

Cyril loved hockey, and it almost always worked to distract him if he was being surly.

"No, he took a scholarship to BU"—which was Boston University—"instead," Cyril said, and sighed. "That'll put them in solid shape for the Beanpot. Looks like we're going to be stuck with that green sophomore in the net this season."

Emily shook her head sympathetically. "I'm sorry. That's too bad. I hope he turns out to be better than you think."

Cyril nodded, looking mournful.

There was a rumbling sound as the school bus drove towards them, slowing to a stop at the corner. Emily and Bobby both ran to get on board, because their regular driver, Mrs. O'Toole, got very impatient if anyone kept her waiting. Since she and Bobby were the only two kids, other than Bobby's big brother and sister, who lived on the peninsula, the bus made just one stop in the area every day, before trundling off to other parts of town.

The junior high took students from several neighboring towns and was *so* much bigger than her Bailey's Cove elementary school had been. She had thought, when school started, that she wouldn't know much of anyone, but there were more children of professors and other Bowdoin College employees than she expected, so she saw a fair number of familiar faces in the halls every day.

It was also the first time she had ever gone to the same school as her friend Karen, and they had a lot of the same classes together, too. So it was fun to be able to sit next to each other and hang out every day. Because of going to different elementary schools, they had been inclined to have more of a "let's do something this weekend" friendship. Spending more time together was great. Unfortunately, the only classes she had with Bobby were science and language arts.

When she got to her homeroom, Karen was already sitting in the back row, listening to her iPod.

Karen's father was a music professor, and her mother was an artist, so Karen was pretty much into *anything* creative. The school really didn't want them to use iPods or cell phones, but they weren't required to put them away until the homeroom bell rang, and they could take them out again at lunch, if they wanted. Lots of people tried to text under their desks during classes, but Emily didn't do it because everyone else always seemed to get caught—and she didn't want to get in trouble.

Emily plopped her knapsack onto her desk and sat down. "What are you listening to?"

"Sun Ra," Karen said.

Emily had no idea who Sun Ra was, but Karen loved jazz, so it was probably some jazz musician. And most likely, Sun Ra was a pianist or a saxophonist, because those were two of Karen's favorite instruments to play. "Would I like him—or her?" Emily asked.

Instead of answering, Karen took out one of her ear buds and held it out. Emily listened for about thirty seconds, and then made a face.

"Kind of screechy," she said.

Karen nodded, turning off the iPod, and tucked it into her own knapsack. "Yeah, but he was all innovative and stuff, you know? So I like to listen, and figure out what he was trying to do."

That made perfect sense, because when her parents took her to art museums, Emily made a point of taking time to look at all of the paintings she *didn't* like, to see what she thought, and why.

"Are your parents still upset?" Karen asked.

Because, naturally, Emily had called her up the night before to tell her about her adventure with Zack. "Not really," she said. "Although I'm not supposed to go underneath cars that might fall down anymore."

"They are *so* unreasonable," Karen said.

Emily grinned. Yeah, the next thing she knew, they would be telling her not to play in traffic, or fly kites in lightning storms, and other mean stuff like that. "One thing, though," she said. "That purple shirt is, like, *wrecked*."

"Good!" Karen said instantly. "Now, you can get a more interesting shirt."

Her purple shirt had been very plain, but she liked it. She could just put it on, and then go about her day without giving it any more thought. Karen—who had long brown hair that she parted in the middle, and very pale white skin, since her mother always made her put on, like, *60* SPF sunscreen—cared a lot more about clothes than Emily did. Sometimes, she even read fashion magazines and stuff like that. They *did* both agree on Converse sneakers, although Emily preferred high-tops to low-tops. The plain black ones were the best, but she had to admit that the multicolored, patterned ones were kind of excellent, too. Karen also liked the patterned ones, but her favorites were her bright pink low-tops.

"I bet you'll get another shirt exactly like it, though," Karen said.

Emily laughed. "I bet I will, too," she said.

4

Emily had only been going to the junior high school for a couple of weeks now, but so far, she mostly liked it. Her teachers were nice, and the classes were okay, and maybe even a little bit interesting. The school seemed huge, after going to a tiny elementary school, where she had known everyone since she was five years old, but people were mostly friendly.

There were only two other African-American students in the whole school—twins, who were in the ninth grade. She hadn't met them, but she had seen them in the hall a couple of times. There were a few Asian kids, maybe five others who were Latino, and about ten students who were Native American, mostly from the Penobscot tribe. Other than that, the school was almost completely Caucasian, which wasn't unusual in Maine. Emily sometimes felt guilty that she even *noticed*, but she couldn't help it.

Her vocabulary test was really easy, and luckily,

she had finished all of her homework the night before because they had a pop quiz on the metric system in math class. In Spanish, they weren't doing much more than saying "*Hola,*" and "*¿Cómo está usted?*" so far, and she was kind of bored; but her teacher was starting at the beginning because some of the people in the class needed to catch up. In gym class, they played soccer, which wasn't her favorite thing to do, but no one kicked her in the shins by accident or knocked her down, so that counted as a good day in physical education, as far as she was concerned.

That afternoon, she was sitting in social studies class, trying to concentrate on a lecture about Ancient China, even though she was feeling sleepy after eating two pieces of pizza for lunch. Not very good pizza—the crust was way too thick, and there wasn't enough cheese—but she had been pretty hungry after running around on the soccer field and ate everything on her tray, even the too-warm fruit cocktail. She had also taken two trips up to the little salad bar, and filled her plate both times.

To try and wake up, she drew a few quick sketches—of Josephine, of Zack, and of a sailboat darting across the ocean. Teachers had never liked it when they caught her drawing in class, but she was convinced that it triggered a different part of her brain—and invariably perked her up.

She wasn't happy with the way the sail turned out—it looked really fake—so she tried again, emphasizing the curve and the way the wind was affecting the cloth. But she *still* didn't like the results, and turned to a new page in her notebook.

Oh, and social studies. She needed to pay attention to social studies. They were talking about Confucianism, and Keith, one of the guys in her class, had already raised his hand twice to say, "Mr. Lambert, I'm confused about Confucianism." Since everyone laughed, Emily assumed he had been kidding, but judging from Keith's expression, she thought he might have been serious the first time he said it. Mr. Lambert promptly went into great detail about governance and morality and the meritocracy—and most of her classmates looked either bored, or just plain intimidated.

Suddenly, there was a familiar scratching sound on the classroom window, and Emily gave some serious thought to hiding underneath her desk. Mostly, Emily thought that Zack was *perfect*—but, yes, he did have one bad habit. Somehow, by hook or crook, he had managed to get out of the house and trot over to the school to visit her, more days than not.

This was only the seventh day of school, and he had already shown up on five of them.

She would either see his white furry head pop up in a window or peek through the door from the hallway—or, out of the blue, a teacher would sigh and say, "Miss Feingold, you seem to have a visitor, *again*." A couple of her teachers thought it was funny when it happened, but most of them seemed to find it annoying—which was pretty reasonable.

Once he realized that she had noticed him, Zachary barked.

"Look, it's the Canine Avenger!" one of the boys in her class shouted, and almost everyone laughed.

Her teacher, Mr. Lambert, sighed. "Miss Feingold, the more times this happens, the less interesting it is."

Right. She glanced across the aisle at Karen, who scribbled a note and flipped it onto her desk.

"*No, it's still interesting*," the note said in Karen's tiny, sloppy handwriting.

Emily felt the same way, but she had enough sense not to say so aloud, so she just nodded.

Zack barked again, and one of the guys sitting near the window opened it partway. Zack took immediate advantage of this and squirmed through the opening. He landed on the floor with a thud and trotted over to her, looking very pleased with himself. Then, he sat down next to her desk and lifted his paw—which Emily automatically shook.

"It's all very well and good that you have a pet, Miss Feingold," her teacher said, his expression rather cross. "But you are going to need to remove him from the room immediately. Not only is he ruining our lesson, but there may be children who are allergic and I don't want you to endanger them."

Right on cue, at least five people in the room coughed loudly, and a few more fake-sneezed—and everyone laughed again.

Emily nodded and quickly stuffed her notebook and textbook into her knapsack; she gestured for Zack to follow her.

Mr. Lambert wrote out a pass to the office and handed it to her. "I'm willing to overlook this today, but see that he stays home from now on."

"Yes, sir," Emily said, and put the hall pass carefully in her pocket.

Once they were safely out in the corridor, Emily bent down to give Zack a big hug. Yes, he shouldn't have come over to the school again, but that didn't mean she wasn't *really* happy to see him.

"How did you get out, anyway?" she asked.

Zack wagged his tail at her, and she had a sudden

and very clear image in her mind of a torn screen window in the little sunroom at their house.

She stared at Zack. "You jumped through the *screen*? You shouldn't have done that—you might have gotten hurt." And, on top of that, her parents might be mad when they found out, since they were going to have to buy a new screen.

Zack let out a happy wiggle, and she knew she was right. That was *exactly* what he must have done this time. After that, he must have run the entire three or four miles over to the school, and crossed lots of roads—which was scary because there would have been so many cars around.

"You can't do that, Zack," she said. "It's not safe for you to be around traffic like that. And what if Josephine got out?"

Zachary cocked his head at her curiously.

She expected him to understand every word she said, but communicating with images seemed to work better. So she closed her eyes and pictured Josephine ambling happily into the sunroom and then jumping up on the windowsill. Her cat sniffed at the screen and then vaulted outside, scampering off into the yard. Emily then imagined herself walking into the sunroom and gasping in horror and despair as she saw Josephine running away.

Then, she opened her eyes and looked at Zack, who ducked his head guiltily.

"You really have to stay home when I'm at school," she said, "okay?"

She had a new image of Josephine wandering into the sunroom, jumping onto the windowsill and yawning with the greatest of boredom. Then, her cat leaped over onto the sofa, curled up in the afternoon sunshine, and went to sleep.

And Emily had no idea whether that was what had happened—or if it was just wishful thinking.

She felt embarrassed about walking Zachary down the corridor, especially when she passed a group of ninth graders who were amused at her expense. But the jokes they made seemed good-natured—they said things like "That is one funny-looking seventh grader!"—so she didn't take it personally.

When she walked into the main office, two of the three administrative assistants smiled, and the other one frowned.

"Well, it looks like your friend misses you when you're gone all day," one of them, Ms. Petrossi, said.

Emily nodded sheepishly.

When she was shown into the principal's office,

Mrs. Wilkins was sitting behind her desk, waiting for her. Mrs. Wilkins dressed very conservatively and wore her hair up in a bun, but when she wasn't working, she trained for triathlons, so she was very fit and energetic.

"Considering that it's only the second week of school, we're getting to know each other awfully well," Mrs. Wilkins said wryly.

Emily nodded. "I'm sorry. He's just really smart, and keeps figuring out how to get out somehow."

Zachary seemed to be extremely happy to see Mrs. Wilkins, and he trotted around the desk to greet her.

Mrs. Wilkins patted him. "He's a lovely dog, Emily. Unfortunately, it's not only disruptive to have him here, but you're also missing a lot of time in class."

"I know," Emily said, and reached for her cell phone. "Is it okay if I call one of my parents to come get him?"

When her principal nodded, Emily checked the clock on the wall and saw that it was just past one thirty. She was pretty sure that her father was teaching a class about the Reconstruction right now, but that her mother was only having office hours, so she dialed her number first.

"Is anything wrong?" her mother asked uneasily when she picked up.

"I'm in the, um, principal's office," Emily said.

Although that was probably not a really good way to start, because her mother gasped.

"I mean, Zack's here again," Emily elaborated.

Her mother sighed. "Ah. Okay. How did he get out this time?"

Teleported, maybe? Unless he really had found his way through a torn screen in the sunroom. "I don't know," Emily said. "But I'm sort of worried that if he left a window open or something, Josephine might have gotten out, too."

Her mother sighed again. "Well, let's hope that she's too sensible for that."

Or, if Josephine wasn't sensible, that she was too *lazy*.

Once she had finished talking to her mother, who was going to come over right away to get Zack, she handed the phone to Mrs. Wilkins, and tried not to eavesdrop on their brief conversation; but the word "disruptive" definitely came up again.

After the phone conversation was over, Mrs. Wilkins wanted her to leave Zack with one of the office secretaries and return to class immediately. Emily wasn't crazy about the idea, but she reluctantly handed the leash to Ms. Petrossi, patted Zack's head, and asked him to stay. But, as soon as she took one step away from him, Zachary got so agitated and nervous—and noisy—that Mrs. Wilkins decided to allow her to wait until her mother got there to pick him up.

So she sat in a chair in the main office, next to two eighth graders who had gotten in a scuffle during gym class and were waiting to see the principal, too.

Zachary looked at the boys suspiciously for a moment. Then, he yawned and stretched out on the carpet, resting his head on her sneaker.

"Cool dog," one of the boys said.

"Thank you," Emily said. She reached down to pat Zack's head, and he wagged his tail once before going back to sleep. "Big fight?"

The two boys looked at each other and shrugged.

"No, we were just being jerks," one of them said.

The other boy nodded. "He kicked me during soccer, and I got mad."

"I *tripped*," the first boy said.

The other boy nodded again. "Well, yeah, I know that *now*."

Mrs. Wilkins came out again and summoned

them into her office, which left Emily by herself in the waiting area. Zack's fur was a little tangled near his right ear, and she wished she had a comb to fix it, but he was sound asleep and probably didn't want to be bothered, anyway.

So she took out her notebook and made another attempt to draw a sailboat streaking through the waves. For some reason, it still looked like something an eight-year-old would sketch, and she stared at the page in frustration. Maybe her mistake was trying to do the entire thing at once. It might make sense to work on the *components*, first, and then put them together in a full drawing later. The hull. The mast. The sail itself.

If she was trying to capture *motion*, and suggest strong winds, maybe the key was to work on the waves. Then, she could add the sailboat, knifing through the water. Although if a sailboat was too hard, maybe she should just try drawing a buoy, being buffeted by waves. It was the same basic concept, artistically, but probably not quite as demanding, and maybe she could learn how to—

Zack's eyes flew open, and he scrambled up. He sniffed the air intently, raising his front paw in the air.

Emily found herself feeling tense and anxious, although she wasn't sure why, and she jumped to her feet, too.

Somewhere in the school, there was something seriously wrong!

5

Zachary tore out of the main office, and Emily chased after him. She could hear at least two people yelling, "Hey, where are you going?" and "Come back!" but there was no time to stop and explain. As they dashed past a teacher, he yelled, "No running in the halls!" at them.

Emily wasn't sure where they were going, but if Zack was going to keep leading her on chases like this, she was going to have to ask her parents if they could buy her some good running sneakers with decent traction. Her high-top Converses weren't really designed for this much activity.

Zachary seemed to be taking her towards the gymnasium, and she picked up her pace, slipping and sliding a little as she tried to keep up. But, no, they were going right on by the gym, and down towards the auditorium.

"What are we doing?" she asked, out of breath.

The only image she got back was the two of

them running down the corridor, so that one wasn't a news flash.

Once they got there, Zack ran headlong into the auditorium doors—which must have been locked, because when he rammed into them, they didn't budge. He panted uncertainly and looked up at Emily for help.

"I think it's closed up," she said, peering through the narrow window in one of the doors.

All she could see inside were long, dark rows of seats, with the broad stage above. The stage was dark, too, except for some slight illumination from two exit signs.

"Zack, I really think it's deserted," she said.

Her dog pawed frantically at the door, so he clearly did not agree.

She tried the handle, and to her surprise, the door swung open, sending a shaft of light into the darkened theater. To be more accurate, the dark, quiet, and *empty* theater.

"Hello?" she said tentatively.

"Is someone there?" a shaky female voice—a *tearful* voice—called, from somewhere near the stage.

"Yeah," Emily said. "Sorry. I didn't mean to

bother you. I just—" Just what? "Well, the door was open."

"Can you help me?" the girl asked. "I think I broke my leg."

Whoa. Emily propped the door open, using the small metal slide to keep it in place. Then, she walked cautiously down the aisle, towards the stage.

Zachary was already trotting ahead of her, and she followed him.

It was hard to see well in the dim light, but there was a girl lying on the floor below the stage, her leg clearly misshapen.

"Wow," Emily said. "What happened?"

The girl had obviously been crying, but she wiped her sleeve across her eyes, and when she spoke her voice sounded stronger. "I forgot my knapsack here after choir practice this morning. So I came back at lunch to get it, and I kind of fell, when I jumped off the stage."

Kind of *totally* fell, based upon how swollen and crooked her leg looked.

"I was trying to crawl up the aisle, to get out of here," the girl said, her voice shaking again. "But it hurt too much."

"I'll go get help," Emily promised.

Zack started up the aisle with her, but she motioned for him to stay.

"No, I'll be right back," she said. "You stay and keep, um—" She looked at the girl uncertainly.

"Charlotte," the girl said.

Emily nodded. "Hi. I'm Emily." She turned to Zack. "Stay and keep Charlotte company, okay?"

She immediately got an image of them racing down the halls again, towards the office, but she shook her head and imagined Zack sitting comfortingly next to Charlotte, while she patted him, instead.

Zack made a small sound of dog protest, but then flopped down on the floor next to Charlotte, who did, indeed, start patting him.

"Wow," Charlotte said, sounding impressed. "That was neat. I would swear you guys were just having a conversation."

"Well, um, he's a really good dog," Emily said. "Anyway, I'll be right back."

She hurried up the aisle, planning to go back to the main office and tell Mrs. Wilkins or the school nurse. But it occurred to her that the gymnasium was closer, and gym teachers were usually pretty smart about injuries.

So she ran to the gym, where Coach Quindlen

was supervising a bunch of eighth graders, who were playing volleyball. Coach Quindlen had lots of red, curly hair, and generally spoke so loudly that people could probably hear her down in *Portland* whenever she raised her voice.

"Excuse me, Coach?" Emily asked politely. She wasn't even sure what sports her gym teacher coached at the school, but they had been told during their first phys ed class to call her "Coach," and *only* "Coach."

Coach Quindlen frowned at her. "You are on the field of play, Emily Feingold. And—why aren't you in class?"

Emily took two steps backwards, so that she was on the sidelines, instead of the court itself. "Charlotte fell in the auditorium, Coach. I think she broke her leg—it's all twisted."

Coach Quindlen frowned and then blew her whistle. "Mary Kristoff, front and center!"

One of the girls stopped playing immediately and jogged over, her ponytail bobbing behind her.

Coach Quindlen handed her the whistle. "You're in charge. The Red Team is still on serve, and is up ten to four."

Mary nodded and put the whistle around her neck.

Once Emily and Coach Quindlen went into the auditorium, everything happened fast. Coach Quindlen had stopped to grab an instant ice pack on the way, and once she had assessed the scene, she quickly summoned the school nurse and called for paramedics, too.

In due course, Mrs. Wilkins also appeared, and to Emily's surprise, her mother showed up, too.

"Where've you been?" her mother asked, sounding much more curious than annoyed.

Emily pointed at Charlotte, who had just had an air splint put on her leg and was now being bundled onto a gurney. Apparently, the preliminary diagnosis was that she had dislocated her knee, and Emily couldn't help shuddering at the thought of how much something like that must hurt.

As the paramedics wheeled her away, Charlotte gave her a thumbs-up, which Emily returned.

By now, it was almost time for school to be dismissed, so Mrs. Wilkins said that it would be okay for her to leave for the day. While her mother took Zack out to the car, Emily went to her locker to get her books and see if she could find Bobby, so that they could give him a ride, too.

Luckily, she ran into him in the hall as classes let out for the day and saw Karen, too; so she was able to tell both of them what had happened, and get her homework assignments for social studies, as well as the science class she had missed.

Then, she and Bobby walked outside to meet her mother in the parking area where parents dropped off and picked up students every day.

"Is it okay if we give Bobby a ride home?" Emily asked. "So he doesn't have to ride the bus?"

Her mother nodded. "Sure. But I want you to ride back over to the college with me afterwards, so I can teach my four o'clock."

Emily wasn't about to start an argument in front of Bobby, but she and her parents had been battling over whether she was old enough to stay home by herself for *weeks* now. Her parents said no; Emily said very definitely, one thousand percent, *yes*. Since she was always out-voted, she would either end up having to spend afternoons in one of her parents' offices studying, or there would be a big deal of making arrangements for her to go to a friend's house, where she would be sure to be supervised by grown-ups at all times.

Personally, Emily thought her parents were *way* too strict about it, but she figured she should wait and press the issue after she officially turned twelve on Saturday.

"I was going to work on the boat this afternoon," Bobby said as he got into the backseat, put on his seat belt, and then patted Zack. "Maybe Emily could come and hang out?"

Her mother hesitated, because she didn't like it when Emily spent time at the docks, since she thought it was a potentially *unsavory* atmosphere—whatever that meant. "Are either of your parents going to be there?"

Bobby shrugged. "I don't know. Dad's hauling traps today, and I'm not sure when he'll be back. And Mom'll be at the pound, probably."

Bobby's father was a lobsterman, and his mother ran a small lobster pound, where all of the locals would go to buy lobsters and crabs and whatever else had been freshly caught.

"But my aunt will be around for sure, working on her gear," Bobby said. "Couple of my cousins might be there, too." His aunt Martha had been the captain of a commercial fishing boat for years, but there were so many new rules and regulations about groundfishing off the Maine coast that she mostly focused on lobstering these days.

Emily knew her mother was too polite to say that she thought most of Bobby's relatives were unruly and rambunctious—which they were. But her mother also thought they were sometimes very bad influences, and Emily didn't agree with that part at all. She *liked* the Percivals. They were always full of energy and fun, and it always made her wish that she was part of a big family, instead of being an only child.

That is, if she *was* an only child. She assumed she was, but sometimes, she couldn't help wondering if she *did* have real siblings somewhere, and would never get to meet them, or even find out who they were.

When they got to her house, Emily ran inside to make sure that Josephine hadn't gotten out. It was a *huge* relief to find her in the den, sound asleep on the love seat, on top of the morning newspaper.

Somehow, Emily wasn't shocked to see that the screen in the sunroom was, in fact, torn, and that was probably exactly how Zachary had gotten out. She shut the window, just to make sure that he—and Josephine—didn't get any bright ideas.

Then, while her mother made a couple of phone calls, and Bobby sat at the kitchen table with some brownies and milk, Emily went upstairs to change into an old Red Sox sweatshirt and some cargo pants. When they worked on the boat, she always ended up getting sawdust and everything all over her clothes.

She wasn't sure why Bobby had recently decided he wanted to build a boat, but it was the most enthusiastic she had ever seen him about any project. Before he started, he had even asked his mother and father if they could take him to a bookstore. His parents were so surprised and pleased that they bought him a whole stack of books on boatbuilding, and his mother took him to get his first library card, too. Bobby still wasn't very good about his homework, but he spent *hours* pouring over his boat books and taking notes and drawing complicated diagrams and blueprints.

Since her mother was running late and had to get back to campus in time for her next class, she agreed that it would be all right for them to walk, with Zack, down to the marina. Emily promised to be careful, and check in, and to call if it started getting *at all* dark when they were finished and she needed a ride home.

Before they headed down to the boatyard, Emily made sure that Zack had had some water and a couple of dog biscuits. There wasn't much traffic, because there were very few year-round residents on the peninsula. Most of the houses belonged to summer people, who all seemed to be very rich—and didn't spend much time in Maine. So, more often than not, the neighborhood was pretty deserted.

Most of Emily's neighbors, like the Peabodys and the Henriks, were retired, and Bobby and his big brother and sister were the only other kids who lived anywhere nearby. So the neighborhood was pretty quiet, but everyone was very friendly and sociable—except for Mrs. Griswold.

Mrs. Griswold was a widow, who lived in a small cottage about halfway between Emily's and Bobby's houses. There were lots of crazy rumors about her, all over town, including people saying that she had a shotgun to keep people away from her property, and that she had killed her husband. Emily's parents had told her that he actually died in a terrible car accident, so Emily didn't believe that rumor, but she thought the one about the shotgun might be true.

All she knew for sure was that Mrs. Griswold was really mean and walked with a cane. Sometimes, she rode an old black bicycle around town, and it always looked very painful.

Bobby was afraid of Mrs. Griswold, but also intrigued by her, because he was *always* eager to walk past her house and see what might happen. Emily, on the other hand, just tried to keep a very low profile.

For some reason, Zack seemed to really like Mrs. Griswold. When they had first gotten him, she had called up a couple of times to complain that he barked too much, but if they ran into her, he always greeted her with an enthusiastic wag of his tail. And, strangely enough, Mrs. Griswold almost seemed to *smile* at him, once in a while. It was more a tiny twitch of the lips than a full smile, but Emily had definitely noticed that Mrs. Griswold wasn't *quite* as mean when Zack was around.

"What do you think Mrs. Griswold does all day?" Bobby asked, as they walked down the road. "Sit inside and think lots of bad stuff about everyone?"

Emily shook her head. "I think she sits inside and feels *sad*."

Bobby looked doubtful. "Maybe. But I kind of think she's in there totally *plotting* against us and stuff." Then, his expression brightened. "Want to throw a rock at her door and then run away really fast?"

"*No*," Emily said. "We're not going to throw a rock."

Bobby hesitated, since he had already picked one up and was in the process of drawing his arm back. "Why?"

There were about a thousand good reasons not to do it. "Well, for one thing, Zack wouldn't like it," Emily said.

"Oh." Bobby instantly dropped the rock. "Okay, then, we won't. But we shouldn't feel like we have to *hide* all the time, instead of, you know, walking by whenever we want. I mean, we live here, too."

Yeah, that was probably fair. "I don't want to bother her," Emily said. "If she wants to be private, I figure we should just leave her alone."

Bobby shrugged. "I guess so. But it seems like she's mean to *us*, not the other way around."

"Well," Emily said, "maybe—"

Just then, there was a loud creaking sound, and they both stopped to look over at the house.

The front door was opening!

6

Mrs. Griswold limped out onto her front porch, wearing a floppy black sweater and black pants.

"Where's her pointed hat?" Bobby whispered.

Emily kind of wanted to laugh, but she elbowed him instead.

Mrs. Griswold started to open her mailbox, but then stopped when she noticed them standing in the road. "Here, now!" she said crossly. "What do you two think you're doing out there?"

Emily looked at Bobby, who she could tell wanted to run away almost as much as she did.

"Um, we're, well, we, um, you see," she started.

Mrs. Griswold looked very impatient. "Spit it out, child! I don't bite."

Actually, people in town said that she *did*.

Emily tried to think of something to say, but Mrs. Griswold made her so nervous that her mind was a blank. "We, uh—we're taking a walk. With my dog."

"Well, go on with you, then," Mrs. Griswold said. "The last thing I need is a bunch of children lollygagging about."

Right.

Unfortunately, Zack—who had been wagging his tail nonstop—had different ideas. He yanked the leash out of Emily's hand, galloped across the street, and sailed over Mrs. Griswold's fence with a graceful leap.

"Oh my goodness," Mrs. Griswold said, looking startled. Then, she frowned at Emily. "Shouldn't you be able to control that animal?"

Okay, he had jumped over her fence and everything, but she didn't like hearing him be described as "that animal." Emily frowned right back at her. "Mrs. Griswold, his name is *Zachary*."

There was a brief, tense silence.

"Yes, of course," Mrs. Griswold said briskly. "All right, then. Go on with you, Zachary."

Instead, Zack bounded up her front steps and stood on the porch, waving his tail back and forth.

Mrs. Griswold sighed. "Oh, *very well*," she said, balanced her weight on her cane, and bent awkwardly to pat him once.

Apparently, that was all Zack had wanted, because he barked in response and then raced back to Emily with another energetic jump over the fence.

Mrs. Griswold shook her head. "Such nonsense," she said, and then took out her mail and limped into the house.

But she had maybe, sort of, kind of smiled.

A little.

Emily looked at Bobby, who shrugged, and they started walking again. Zack seemed to be delighted with himself and practically danced his way along the road.

"That was weird," Bobby said.

"He can actually jump a lot higher than that, I think," Emily said. "That fence is, what, maybe three feet?"

Bobby laughed. "Not the *fence*. I meant Mrs. Griswold acting almost like she had a personality or something."

"Zack likes her," Emily said, "and I think that makes her like *him*."

"It's still weird," he said. "But, hey, she didn't shoot us, right?"

That was true—there had been no gunplay whatsoever.

As they approached the marina, Zack's mood

seemed to improve even more, and he wagged his tail so hard that his whole body shook. Which was a relief, because the first couple of times she had taken him down to the cove, he had been *really* afraid of the docks. Emily was almost sure it was because it reminded him of his first owners, who had been two really lazy and unpleasant brothers who were fishermen somewhere up on the Mid Coast.

Now, though, he really seemed to enjoy going down there. Phil, who owned the boatyard next to the main wharf, always gave him pieces of beef jerky, which probably added to Zack's enthusiasm.

Most of the boats probably wouldn't come into the harbor until near sunset, so the docks were pretty quiet. There were a few people around cleaning their boats, checking the engines, preparing bait, and doing other housekeeping chores. As they walked across the parking lot, almost everyone waved at them or called out hellos.

The marina for recreational speedboats and sailboats and everything was off to their left, in the most sheltered part of the cove. That was the most touristy area and included two restaurants, an ice cream shop, a small motel with water views, and Crowley's Sea Shack, where people could buy fried clams and lobster rolls and clam cakes and all. It was always very crowded in the summer, but in the off-season, there usually wasn't much going on.

Next to that was a combination boatyard and small lumberyard, where boat owners and fishermen could shop for supplies and arrange for storage or repairs. The harbormaster's cabin was next to that, built up on a platform with windows on all sides, so that the harbormaster and his assistants would always have a good view of the entire cove. To the right of that were the small wharves for working fishermen and lobstermen, including a few long, slim wooden docks. Most of the lobster boats had assigned moorings out in the sound, and it was easy to tell when a boat was out at sea, because a small skiff or dory would be tied to the mooring instead.

Bobby's family's lobster pound was around a bend in the coastline, just out of sight. It was built right onto the waterfront, with big tanks inside that pumped seawater in and out nonstop, to keep the lobsters and other seafood fresh. Often, the boats would stop there on their way in from a day of hauling traps and immediately unload some of their catch, before cruising into the main section of the cove.

The lobster pound had a small industrial kitchen, and when Mrs. Percival was in the mood, she would fire up the fryer or start steaming a bunch of clams. More often than not, she had a big pot of chowder simmering on a back burner, too, and if things were quiet, she would usually bake a few loaves of sourdough bread and maybe a couple of blueberry pies, too. Once Emily had become a vegetarian—which all of the Percivals thought was odd—Mrs. Percival had always made a point to have some homemade vegetable soup or corn chowder available, so that she could enjoy casual meals with the rest of them.

Bobby's aunt Martha was over on one of the docks, where her boat, *Lady's Choice*, was tied up. It was a pretty neat-looking boat, with a bright red hull and a red roof on the tiny wheelhouse. There were lobster traps piled in front of her, and it looked like she was busy replacing the hog rings on a couple of them. She was wearing rubber boots, thick canvas pants, a grey sweatshirt, and an old Red Sox cap with a big brown ponytail sticking out of the back.

"Hi, Aunt Martha!" Bobby said, and waved.

"Hey, kids!" she yelled back. Aunt Martha was hearty and gruff, but she was also the president of the local fishermen's cooperative and spent a lot of time talking about things like environmental sustainability and revitalizing the industry. She put her pliers down on top of the nearest trap and walked over to meet them. "Just got off the phone with your mother a little while ago, Emily."

Somehow, that didn't come as a surprise. "You're supposed to keep an eye on us, right?" Emily guessed.

Aunt Martha nodded. "You bet. Told her I'd give you a ride home in time for supper—unless I have to take both of you to the emergency room to have all of your fingers reattached."

Oh, no. "Did my mother think that was funny?" Emily asked.

"No, she did not," Aunt Martha said with a big smile. "Not even one little bit." Then, she turned to Bobby. "What's on the docket today, sport?"

"Maybe some more framing, but mostly sanding and planing," he said.

"No saws, machetes, axes, knives, swords, rocket launchers, flammable liquids, or hazardous materials?" Aunt Martha asked.

Bobby grinned and shook his head. "Nope."

"All right," she said. "You kids holler if you need help." She gave Zack a firm, affectionate pat on the back. "If they're overcome by fumes of some kind and fall to the ground in jumbled little heaps, you come get me right away, sailor boy."

Emily laughed and pictured herself having a ferocious, slashing sword duel with Bobby—and Zack must have gotten the gist of what she was thinking, because he instantly stiffened and looked at her with alarm.

Ooops. Emily promptly revised the thought, and this time she imagined a much more gentle, theatrical duel, and made sure that she and Bobby had big smiles on as they put the swords safely away in leather scabbards.

It was kind of funny that Zack seemed to be very relieved by that.

Aware that Bobby was watching them, Emily felt her cheeks get hot.

"Um, sorry," she said.

"Were you, like, talking to him?" he asked.

"Not on purpose," she said. "Sometimes it just, you know, *happens*."

He nodded, apparently not creeped out—or even *surprised*—by any of that, as he pulled open the big wooden doors to the Percival family storage shed.

At this stage, his boat was mostly pieces of wood, blueprints, and small cardboard models, which he kept making to test various patterns and designs. Emily had drawn all sorts of sketches of rowboats and dinghies and skiffs, too, which Bobby would study at length. Then, he would make suggestions, and she would redo the drawings until she had come up with something they both liked.

Bobby's father had made a worktable for him out of an old wooden door placed on top of three sawhorses. The door was clamped in place, so the table was pretty sturdy; and as long as he was very careful, Bobby had been given permission to use his grandfather's old tools.

The boat was going to be a twelve-foot skiff, with three board seats. If it worked, it could be used with a little outboard motor, or even a sail, if Bobby decided to add a mast. He was using special marine plywood, and instead of putting it together with epoxy or other fancy glue, he was planning to nail and caulk it together the old-fashioned way.

The only parts that had been assembled so far were five rectangular frames, which curved near the front of the boat and were shaped more like trapezoids in that section. They were set up perpendicular to the worktable and connected by a long, slim piece of marine plywood, which was the guideline for the keel. The wooden frame that would form the back end of the boat looked the most finished, with beveled edges and everything.

Or, anyway, that was what Emily *assumed*, because she didn't completely understand the process yet.

She saw two long, curved pieces of wood carefully propped against the wall that hadn't been there the last time she'd come down to help. There were also four skinny wooden strips and two slightly thicker ones leaning a few feet away. "Hey, wow, is that going to be the bottom of the boat?" she asked.

Bobby nodded. "Yeah. Dad took me to Kurt's over the weekend"—Kurt worked as Bobby's father's regular sternman in the lobster boat—"and they let me use his jigsaw to cut them." He frowned and pointed to one slightly crooked edge. "I kind of screwed up on that part, but Dad says if I bevel it later, it should be okay."

Since it was a nice day, they carried a card table outside to work on, while Zachary watched every move they made with great interest.

"So, what are we going to do today?" Emily asked.

"I'll use Grandpop's plane on the support strips, and you can help sand them so they're good and smooth?" he suggested.

"Okay," Emily said agreeably.

They had both promised their parents that they would wear safety gear when they worked—which her mother had provided in a large gift box, as her contribution to the project. So they put on little air-filter breathing masks, plastic safety glasses, and their work gloves.

"Sort of feels like we're getting ready to work on plutonium, instead of regular old *wood*," Bobby said, his voice muffled behind his mask.

It *was* silly, but Emily liked putting the gear on, because it felt like part of an important working ritual. She also brought a big towel outside and spread it out on a patch of grass, so that Zack could watch them in complete comfort. Because he was the best dog ever, he would even consent to wearing safety goggles to protect his eyes, too, as long as Emily didn't fasten them tightly.

Sanding could be boring, but Emily liked the way the wood felt afterwards, and it was nice to be outside in the sunshine.

"It'll never float!" someone yelled at them.

It was Larry, Bobby's big brother, jogging past them up on the main road. He was a star on the high school lacrosse team and spent a lot of time running and training every day, no matter what the weather was like.

"Yeah, well, you'll never get to ride in it, dude!" Bobby yelled back.

Larry laughed and kept running.

Emily was pretty envious of people who had siblings—it seemed like they had so much *fun* together.

"It *is* going to float," Bobby said nervously, once his brother was safely out of view, "right?"

Emily nodded. "Absolutely. It's going to be excellent."

Bobby nodded, too, somewhat less confidently, and went back to his planing.

They didn't talk much while they worked, other than vague remarks about school and the new people they were each meeting, and that sort of thing. Just for fun, they tried putting on the planks for the bottom, and Bobby threw his fist up and said, "Yeah!" when it was clear that they were going to fit almost perfectly.

"Hold off and nail when your father is here to double-check?" Emily asked.

Bobby thought about that. "I guess so, yeah. But it looks good, doesn't it?"

It looked *great*.

And Emily was completely convinced that, one day soon, the boat really *was* going to float.

7

At about six thirty, Aunt Martha drove them home, with all of their fingers magically intact, and Zack's paws unwounded, too.

Emily found her mother in the kitchen, where she was watching CNN and husking some fresh corn.

"Did you have fun?" her mother asked.

"Yeah, it was good," Emily said. "I think we're going to put on the bottom part of it soon, and then we'll get to the sides. It's pretty cool." She grinned and held out her hands. "And *look* at my beautiful fingers!"

"Not funny," her mother said.

Well, actually, it was *really* funny—but maybe she wouldn't push it.

"Bobby probably poured ketchup all over his hands and ran into his house screaming," her mother said.

Probably, yeah. Emily laughed. "Unless he used

corn syrup and red food coloring, to make it look more realistic."

Her mother raised her eyebrows. "Do I want to know why you know that particular combination?"

"Halloween, two years ago," Emily said. "When Karen went as a vampire." And had, in fact, looked pretty scary.

Her mother thought about that and then nodded. "Right, I remember. The stains never came out, did they?"

Yeah, that would definitely be one of the downsides to being a vampire. "No," Emily said. "We tried, like, tie-dyeing the shirt, to make it look like the red was *supposed* to be there, but that didn't work, either."

Karen's grandmother, who lived on a tiny island farther up the coast where she spent a lot of time painting seascapes, always gave them projects like that when she came to visit—tie-dyeing, batik, macramé. She has very long, grey hair that she wore in a thick braid down her back, and even in the winter, she often had on leather sandals. As far as Emily could tell, she was an actual, *real* hippie, which was pretty cool.

For supper, they had baked chicken and—in Emily's case—baked tofu with teriyaki sauce, boiled red potatoes, corn on the cob, and a big salad. Dessert was frozen yoghurt, with fresh wild blueberries.

Since her mother had cooked, her father did the dishes, and Emily helped him by putting away the leftovers and drying the pans that wouldn't fit in the dishwasher. Josephine sat on the kitchen table and watched all of this with disgust, while Zachary sniffed around, looking for snacks. The only part of their supper that had interested him was, of course, the chicken, and she gave him a couple of small bites and some to Josephine, too. Which was okay, because they were animals, and meat was what they liked to eat—but she *totally* washed her hands after that.

"Okay. What should we do tonight? A movie, or the Red Sox?" her father asked when they were finished.

Emily thought about that. It was just past eight, so that meant that they were probably somewhere around the top of the fourth inning. "I don't know. I guess it depends on what the score is."

"Good point," her father said.

They went into the den, where her mother was grading papers at the little antique desk in the corner. Zachary and Josephine both followed them into the room, and Zack flopped down on the rug, while Josephine sprawled across the love seat, so that there would be no room for anyone else to sit down. For a really small cat, she had always been good at taking up *a lot* of space.

"How are you coming along?" Emily's father asked her mother. "We were thinking either a movie or the game."

"Check the score first," her mother said instantly.

Her father turned on the television, and they saw that it was eight to nothing—and the Red Sox were losing.

"Well, okay," he said, and turned on the DVD player. "I guess that makes it easier to decide."

It only took a couple of minutes of debating—which Emily mostly ignored, because she liked almost *all* movies—for her parents to agree upon what they were going to watch. They ended up putting in *Ghostbusters*, which was one of her father's favorites, because he always said it was "so New York."

When the movie was over, her mother switched to the baseball game, and they saw that the Red Sox were now winning, ten to eight. But the bases were loaded, and the Tampa Bay batter promptly hit a double to the gap, and the Red Sox were losing eleven to ten.

"Never mind," her mother said, and turned it off again.

It was pretty clear that deciding to watch the movie, instead of baseball, had been a *really* good idea.

The next morning, Emily and her mother took Zachary to the vet for a checkup and some booster shots. When she had originally found him, he had been injured *and* had pneumonia, so they had to make sure that he was staying nice and healthy now. Emily wanted to be a veterinarian herself when she grew up, and the people had always been really nice at the vet's office about answering her questions and letting her observe things. She was hoping that when she was older, she could maybe work as an intern at the clinic after school.

When they got there, one of the technicians weighed Zack on a special scale. He wasn't at all fat, but he was really big, and he now weighed ninety-six pounds. Emily wasn't sure how much he was supposed to weigh, but she was definitely glad that his ribs weren't sticking out anymore.

They waited in the examining room for a few

minutes, until their vet came in with a big smile on his face.

"How is our intrepid friend today?" Dr. K. asked, after they all exchanged hellos. His real name was Dr. Kasanofsky, but everyone called him Dr. K. "That was quite an article in the paper this week."

The picture had been great, too, and both Mr. and Mrs. Henrik had given long and complimentary interviews. Her father had brought home several copies, so that she could save them. "Mostly, he seems really happy," Emily said.

"He certainly *looks* happy," Dr. K. said, and patted him on the head.

Zachary didn't really like being up on the table—as far as Emily could tell, he was kind of afraid of heights—but he wagged his tail and stood there obediently while he was examined.

"That sounds very good," Dr. K. said, after listening to Zachary's heart and lungs with his stethoscope. "How is his appetite?"

"He never stops eating," Emily's mother said wryly.

Dr. K. smiled. "I think I'll put down 'hearty,'" he said, and typed that into the case notes file on his computer. "Are you seeing anything at all unusual?"

Emily was immediately tempted to say, "*Yes*, totally unusual," but she didn't. She must have started to open her mouth as if she were going to speak, though, because her mother and Dr. K. both looked at her.

"What have you noticed, Emily?" Dr. K. asked.

Well, she couldn't say that her dog could read her mind and regularly communicated with her—even though it *was* very unusual. "Um, well," she said, and tried to think of an answer which would make her sound less weird than that. "He comes to school a lot. I mean, we're always sure we've closed him up in the house, but then I'm sitting in class, and he suddenly shows up."

"Maybe it's magic," Dr. K. said. "Perhaps he's flying."

Obviously, he was kidding, but Emily laughed nervously.

"One of my colleagues suggested that we put him in a crate during the day," Emily's mother said, "but I'm not particularly comfortable with that concept—especially for such a big dog."

Emily had overheard her parents discussing the concept of a crate a couple of days earlier—and had been quite outraged by the idea. But, luckily, her parents weren't enthusiastic about it, either.

She tuned out a little while her mother and Dr. K. talked about some ideas to make sure Zachary remained safely inside when they weren't home. There was no way he could fly—she knew that—but what if it turned out that she was wrong? What if—no, that would be so far past *weird* and *unusual* that she wasn't going to waste time thinking about it.

Zack was looking at her intently, and she patted his head. He wagged his tail but kept looking at her. She tried to concentrate, but couldn't come up with any images or messages whatsoever.

Maybe she wasn't focusing strongly enough? So she tried again, but still had no sense of anything other than her *own* thoughts.

Her left arm had started aching, and she rubbed it automatically. It was throbbing pretty intensely, especially between her elbow and wrist, although she couldn't remember having done anything to—*oh*. Okay, now she got it.

She waited until there was a lull in the conversation her mother and Dr. K. were having, and then spoke up. "I think Zack's leg still hurts him sometimes. Could he maybe have arthritis?"

Dr. K. reached out to check Zachary's left foreleg again. "No, he's a young dog, and it wouldn't happen right away like that. And you haven't been seeing any sign of a limp, right?"

Emily shook her head. "No, but he's sometimes—uncomfortable. I mean, he seems that way. As though it hurts him right"—she gestured towards her own arm—"here."

In the end, Dr. K. decided to send them home with ten days' worth of pain medication, which they could give to Zack twice a day, if his leg seemed to be bothering him.

"I'm impressed by how attuned you are to him, Emily," he said, as he wrote out the prescription.

Total understatement, but yeah. "Thank you," she said.

Nervously.

That afternoon, her mother went to a meeting of her kayak club, while Emily and her father went over to the college to swim in the pool for an hour. Well, Emily swam, while her father sat on a wooden bench and read a book.

It was a quiet weekend, in general, which was very relaxing. On Sunday, they went to church and then drove down to Portland to have brunch and spend the afternoon at the art museum. They spent time looking at two new exhibits, one of which focused on a Maine artist who painted landscapes, while the other was a photography exhibit that her father *loved.*

After that, they walked through the Winslow Homer gallery and then went upstairs to check out the French impressionists, which were Emily's favorite. But she mostly liked everything in the museum, except for the cubism—which she thought was too angular and bright and kind of *chilly*—and the ceramics.

Her mother made some really good baked macaroni and cheese for supper, and Emily and her father put together a big salad and a loaf of garlic bread. When they had finished and the dishes were done, Emily sat down at the kitchen table to finish up her homework—after listening to a brief "why do you *always* leave it until the last minute?" lecture from her parents.

Normally, she liked to do her homework upstairs in her room, but her parents sometimes asked her to do it downstairs, so that they could make sure she was concentrating, and not goofing around on the Internet.

So she did all of the algebra equations for math, let her father quiz her on her Spanish vocabulary list, wrote two descriptive paragraphs for language arts, and answered the six questions at the end of the chapter about rock classifications in her science book. Then, she went up to her room—and goofed around on the Internet for a while. Checked her email, sent a few IMs, and watched a few silly comedy videos from various links her friends had sent her.

"Anything shocking?" her father asked, from the door.

Emily turned guiltily—even though the videos were things like people getting hit with pies in the face over and over again. "No. Just, you know, goofy stuff Ronald"—who was one of her cousins—"and Harriet"—who was a friend of hers at school—"sent me."

Her father laughed. "Well, with Ronald, it *could* be shocking."

He was right about that. Ronald was only ten, but he was pretty good at finding ways to get into trouble. "Yesterday, he sent me a video of people's umbrellas blowing out backwards when they were trying to walk in the rain," Emily said. Which sounded stupid, but was really funny when it was twenty or thirty different people, one after the other.

"Well, that sounds pretty harmless," her father

said. He reached down to pat Josephine, who woke up from a sound sleep and leaped over to the windowsill as though he had just done something dreadful. "I don't understand cats, Emily, I really don't."

"She likes to be dramatic," Emily said.

"That's for sure," her father agreed. Then, he tentatively patted Zack, who thumped his tail once without even bothering to open his eyes. "Want to come downstairs for some ice cream, before you go to sleep?"

Emily closed out the website she was on without a second thought. "Definitely!" she said.

Zachary was very excited when he realized that they were going down to the kitchen—which was his favorite room in the house. It was time for him to have his evening painkiller, and Emily carefully mixed it into a tiny scoop of vanilla ice cream, which he finished in about four seconds without seeming to notice that the medication was in there.

She, personally, was going to have some peanut butter cup ice cream, and maybe fudge ripple, too, but those weren't healthy things for Zack to eat. She gave him two dog biscuits, instead. Her father liked ice cream in general, so he ate any flavor that was in the freezer. Her mother had fixed herself a very small dish of nonfat yoghurt, because even though she always said she didn't worry about calories, she actually *did*. But Emily would see her reading books with titles like *Body Image and Your Adolescent* and assumed that she was trying to be a good role model by not talking much about weight and food.

Emily figured that as long as she ate reasonably healthy stuff and got some exercise, she would mostly be okay. Sometimes, though, she was totally full of energy, and other times, she felt like she wanted to sleep for, like, twelve hours. "Growing pains," her father would say. She thought he was kidding, but whenever she was growing a lot, there were days when her bones and muscles actually *did* seem to hurt. She would feel all weird and stiff and achy. Whenever it happened, her mother would run a hot bath for her, and she would stay in there for a *really* long time reading.

Zachary had fallen asleep on the little braided rug near the back door, and he seemed to be dreaming about eating chunks of red meat, which was gross. Anyway, that was what kept popping into her mind, and she knew *she* wasn't the one thinking about that. The best way to clear it out of her head was probably to start a conversation about something else.

"Do I have to be careful about eating too much ice cream, so I don't get fat?" she asked.

"Well, as you get older, your metabolism will change, and it makes sense to be preemptive about—" Her mother stopped, and frowned. "No," she said more carefully. "Of course not. You don't need to worry about that at all."

That was exactly the sort of very cautious answer she had expected, and Emily laughed.

"I think you just set your mother up for that one, Little Emily," her father said, looking amused.

Emily nodded cheerfully. He only called her "Little Emily" once in a while, but she always thought it was funny.

"My senior seminar doesn't end until five tomorrow," her father said, "and your mother has a faculty senate meeting all afternoon."

Emily shrugged, concentrating on her ice cream. "Okay." She had been about to say, "Okay, *whatever*," and maybe even sigh really deeply, but that would just start trouble.

"So, we need to figure out a way to get you over to the campus," her father said. "Maybe we can give you a note so you can take a different bus, and then you can hang out in one of our offices or do your homework in the common room."

Were they really going to go through this again? It had been a big issue ever since school started, and she found it very frustrating. Emily put her spoon down. "What? I still don't get it. Why can't I just come home?"

Her mother sighed. "We've *discussed* this, Emily. We don't want you here after school by yourself."

Emily didn't like to call her a babysitter, because she hadn't been a baby, but when she started kindergarten, her parents had hired a nice retired legal secretary named Mrs. Murphy, who would pick her up from school every day, stay with her all afternoon, and usually fix supper, too.

When Emily was really little, she had just assumed that Mrs. Murphy only came over because she *liked* Emily, and it had been sort of a shock to find out that her parents were *paying* her to do it. Not that she didn't care about Emily, of course, but it was still startling.

But, over the past summer, Mrs. Murphy and her husband had decided that they were tired of the cold weather and long winters in Maine. They had moved to Arizona, where—based upon the postcards and notes she had sent—she was spending a lot of time playing golf.

"I'm going to be *twelve* on Saturday," Emily said, "remember? I don't need a babysitter anymore."

Her mother shook her head. "I'm sorry. Your father and I wouldn't be able to relax, knowing that you were rattling around here by yourself."

"But I won't be by myself," Emily pointed out. "Zack and Josephine will keep me company."

Hearing his name, Zack slapped his tail against the floor—while Josephine took advantage of the distraction to sneak in and start licking some of the ice cream in Emily's bowl.

"They're both wonderful animals," her father agreed, "but I really don't feel comfortable having them in charge until one of them gets a driver's license."

Emily wasn't in the mood to see the humor in that. "Everyone *else's* parents let them stay home alone after school." Which maybe wasn't true, now that she thought about it, but it was too late to back down. "I'm the *only* one who gets treated like a big baby. Even though I'm in *junior high.*"

"We're not really concerned about what other parents are doing," her father said. Which she could have predicted. "We're concerned about *you.*"

"It's not like I'm going to do anything bad," Emily said. "And I wouldn't even be alone that long. I could just do homework and all."

Her mother looked at her watch. "I wonder if it's too late to give Karen's mother a call. Maybe you could spend the afternoon with them."

Emily loved going over to Karen's house—but that wasn't the point. "She has to go to the orthodontist tomorrow."

"Oh." Her mother frowned. "Okay. Well, maybe—"

"Why doesn't Bobby just come over here until you guys get home?" Emily suggested.

Her mother shook her head. "No. Not when your father and I aren't home."

It felt like the older she got, the more *rules* there were. She had always assumed that she would be given a lot more freedom once she was in junior high, but it sure didn't seem to be happening. And as far as she was concerned, her parents always got *way* out of control when it came to being overprotective. "I don't see what the big deal is. I mean, we'd probably just go down to the dock and work on the boat, anyway," Emily said.

Her mother sighed. "I'm not always comfortable with that, either, Emily. I really don't think it's a very wholesome atmosphere for you."

Fishermen and lobstermen could be a little, um, *colorful*, maybe—especially as far as their language was concerned. But Bobby's aunt, or whichever other relative of his was around, was always quick to usher anyone who was behaving badly out of earshot, and usually gave them a cross lecture, too. Mostly, though, everyone down at the wharf was pleasant and polite—at least, when she and Bobby were nearby. Besides, the two of them were usually too busy working on the boat to pay too much attention to whatever else was going on.

Emily frowned. "So, it was okay for me to go down there *Friday*—when Dad was here taking a nap and stuff—but, tomorrow, it would be *bad*?"

Her mother looked tired. "Are we going to have this fight every night for the rest of the school year?"

Boy, that *did* sound tiring. "Probably," Emily said.

Her mother pushed away her mostly uneaten yoghurt. "It's pretty basic. We both want you to come over to the college tomorrow right after school, okay? I'll call the school in the morning and let them know that you'll need to switch to the bus that stops by the campus."

If she were smart, she would probably just nod—and drop the subject, for now. She could always try again another day. But, sometimes, she got tired of *always* losing arguments. Emily put her spoon down, too. "So you're saying you guys don't trust me not to get in trouble, even though I *always* call and say where I am, and Zack'll be with me the whole time. I mean, it's not like I've ever done anything really bad." At least, she didn't *think* she had.

This time, hearing his name, Zack got up and came over to stand next to her.

Emily patted him absentmindedly. But Zack must have been able to tell that she was tense and frustrated, because he rested his muzzle on her knee and looked at her with great concern.

"It's not that we don't trust you," her father said. "We just can't help worrying about you."

Emily frowned. "Do you think I, like, *inherited* bad stuff?"

Her parents looked confused.

"Well, like, my mother was all irresponsible and everything, and gave me up, right?" Emily said. "So maybe I'll be like that, too."

Her mother started to say something, paused, and then shook her head. "First of all, *no*, we don't think that. And second, I think that your mother made a very mature and *responsible* decision, because she wasn't going to be able to take care of you. It's something to *admire*."

Maybe. Except for the part where she hadn't been brave enough to keep in touch or write or call, or even ever send a birthday card. Maybe this year would be different, and a surprise envelope would show up in the mail—but she doubted it.

This was the sort of conversation none of them really liked having, and mostly, they tried to avoid the subject.

"It's harder, around your birthday," her mother said unexpectedly.

Yes. It very definitely was. Emily nodded.

"Well," her mother said, and moved over to hug her—which felt good.

There was no point in asking whether they thought she might get a card this time, because they had no way of knowing, either. So she might as well go back to their original topic.

"When *will* I be old enough to come home by myself, and have you not worry?" Emily asked.

"Old enough for us not to worry?" her father asked. "When you're about a hundred and seventy-eight, maybe?" He paused. "Except I think we would probably still be a little concerned."

Okay, so she had a hundred and sixty years to go.

"Probably, to some degree, when you're thirteen," her mother said, after a moment. "And then, increasingly, once you start high school."

Well, that was specific—even though it seemed sort of arbitrary. How different was being thirteen from being twelve? But it was getting late, and she decided just to nod cooperatively. "Okay. Can I have some more ice cream?" she asked.

Her parents both looked very relieved.

"You bet!" her father said, and opened up the freezer.

When she had finished brushing her teeth and getting ready for bed, she found Zack already asleep on top of her quilt, with his head on her pillow. It was pretty cute, and she laughed.

The sound woke him up and he wagged his tail, but didn't lift his head.

"You look nice and comfortable, but where am *I* going to sleep?" she asked.

He wagged his tail, but still didn't move.

Josephine was over on the windowsill, washing her face. Before Emily had even had time to ask Zack to move over, Josephine had already jumped onto the bed—and onto the pillow, landing directly on his head.

Zack scrambled to his feet, alarmed and confused.

Josephine gave him a small hiss—and then curled up on the pillow herself.

At least there would be a little more room, since a small cat took up a lot less space than a very large dog.

Emily got under the covers, and Zack settled down at the bottom of the bed. Since Josephine appeared to have no interest in leaving the pillow, Emily automatically sent her a visual image of her getting up and moving to a more convenient spot.

Almost immediately, Zack stood uncertainly, looking around the bed for another place to lie down.

"Oh, no," Emily said. "Not you, Zack, you're fine."

He cocked his head at her, looking puzzled.

"I want Josephine to move," she explained. "So that I can lie down, too."

But Zack must just have heard the word "move" because he jumped down to the floor.

Okay, one thing at a time. This animal communication stuff sure got complicated sometimes. She had never had any sense that she could talk to Josephine telepathically, but it might be interesting to *try*.

So she concentrated as hard as she could, creating a visual scene where Josephine gracefully rose from the pillow, stretched happily, and decided to lie down next to her, instead.

But nothing happened.

She tried again, and Josephine just looked at her with unblinking eyes, her tail switching back and forth a little.

"You *do* know what I'm thinking, don't you?" Emily said. "You just don't feel like moving."

Josephine kept looking at her steadily—but there was maybe something a little wicked in her eyes now.

Yeah, that seemed like exactly the right response for a cat to have. And Josephine would probably never share her thoughts with Emily, because she wanted to keep her privacy. That seemed reasonable, too. Although it was also possible that she always listened to the conversations Emily and Zack had—and simply didn't feel like participating.

"Well, at least you don't make sarcastic comments," she said to Josephine—who still had no response.

And luckily, as far as the pillow was concerned, Emily had a trump card: *Josephine only weighed eight pounds*. So Emily just reached down and lifted her up.

Josephine meowed in protest but didn't struggle, and Emily set her down on the quilt, a couple of feet away. Her cat must have thought that being unceremoniously moved was *very* undignified, because she turned her back on Emily and began to wash her face.

Zack was still standing indecisively in the middle of the room, on the red braided rug.

Emily patted the bottom of the bed. "Here, boy," she said.

Zack wagged his tail and jumped back up.

Once both of her pets had finally made themselves comfortable, Emily picked up the book on her bedside table to read for a while. She had just started a new chapter, when she had a weird, vivid image of biting Zack's ear and then chomping down on his leg—and a sense of great amusement for having done so.

Definitely not *her* thought. She peeked over the top of her book at Josephine, who was lying on her back, purring happily—and staring at her.

"Very funny," Emily said.

Josephine purred even more loudly, and then the thoughts washed out of Emily's mind as her cat went to sleep.

Okay. There was one thing that Emily had very definitely learned tonight.

It was possible that, at any given moment, she would rather *not* know what Josephine was thinking.

There was a hurricane coming. Or, anyway, that's what the weather people were saying on television—and in the newspaper and on the Internet and everything. It was called Hurricane Maria—or possibly Tropical Storm Maria, or maybe even Tropical *Depression* Maria—and it was thousands of miles away, somewhere in the Atlantic Ocean. Apparently, the storm was supposed to track directly towards Maine, but it would take another few days to happen.

In Bailey's Cove, people around town were mostly saying, "Yeah, *right.*" Every time there was a new storm down in Bermuda or someplace, the meteorologists in New England all seemed to be convinced that it was heading directly north with frightening speed—and that the entire region was doomed. So this time, as usual, the news was saying that the storm was *definitely* going to strike coastal Maine, and that it was going to be *really bad.*

Or not, since the storm might just spin around

harmlessly in the ocean, or never even get past Florida.

Usually, by the time hurricanes made it all the way up to Maine, all that happened was that it might rain a little. Or it would be windy, and a couple of tree branches might fall down and stuff like that. But that was about it, in Emily's experience.

The last time there had been a real hurricane in Maine was back in the early 1990s, and before that, it might have even been in the *1950s*.

It wasn't that Maine didn't have storms. They had rainstorms, thunderstorms, snowstorms, ice storms—all kinds of storms. But, for whatever reason, hurricanes mostly seemed to run out of steam on their way up north.

That didn't change the fact that as she and her parents made breakfast two days later, the meteorologists were totally excited and seemed very sure that *this* time, it really *was* going to be a huge "storm of the century."

Emily was fixing English muffins for everyone, while her father scrambled eggs and her mother cut up fresh fruit. Zack sat alertly near the stove, in case her father dropped one of the small chunks of cheese he was adding to the eggs. Josephine had apparently decided that it was too early, because the last time Emily had seen her, she was still asleep up on her bed.

She looked at the television screen when they started talking about the extended forecast. "Hey, whoa," she said. "That doesn't look too good for Saturday." In fact, it appeared that the storm was actually going to *hit* right on her birthday, and that the entire weekend was going to be stormy.

Her father shrugged, flipping Zack a piece of cheddar. "When was the last time they were right? It'll probably be sunny and clear."

Boy, she sure hoped so. Since turning twelve was an important birthday, they had spent a fair amount of time talking about something special to do that day. Her first choice has been to go to the water park down near Old Orchard Beach, but it had already closed for the season, so that was out.

Then, she had thought it would be *really* fun to go on a trail ride on horseback up Bradbury Mountain, but her grandparents were planning to fly up from New York; and when it came to nature, they made her father look like Daniel Boone. Plus, both Karen and her friend Harriet had said something to the effect of "um, get up on actual *horses*?" So, her mother had promised that she and Emily could go on a trail ride—her father politely, but eagerly, declined—on some other weekend afternoon before it got too cold. Bobby and Emily's really tiny friend Florence, who was a total jock, was probably going to come on the trail ride, too.

But the main birthday excursion was now going to be a whale-watching cruise on Casco Bay. Her parents and grandparents were coming, along with about ten of her friends. Going whale watching was the kind of thing that local people forgot to do, because it seemed too touristy, but Emily thought it sounded really fun. Supposedly, they had a good chance of seeing whales, sea turtles, sharks, and maybe even some dolphins—which would be neat. Then, they were going to have a birthday picnic on one of the islands out in the Bay before cruising back to Portland right around sunset.

"If it rains on Saturday, we can have a party indoors, and then try to do the cruise next weekend," her mother said.

Emily nodded, since the most important part was being able to spend her birthday with her friends. It didn't really matter *where* they were when they did it.

When she got down to her bus stop, the usual gang of locals was sitting at the picnic table, drinking coffee, and debating about the possibility of the hurricane actually hitting Maine. Today's group was Mr. Washburn, Mr. Bolduc, Mrs. Parsons, and Ms. Benoit, who was considered the best car mechanic in town.

"Nice fresh fritters here, Emily," Mr. Bolduc said. "Would you like one?"

Definitely! Mr. Bolduc was famous for his truly spectacular homemade corn fritters. "Yes, please," Emily said, and happily accepted a still-warm fritter, wrapped in a bright green napkin.

She had only half finished it when she saw Bobby trudging up the road, with his hair unbrushed and seeming half asleep. He usually didn't look alert until at least lunchtime.

"Morning," he mumbled, and they all waved at him.

"Here," Mr. Bolduc said. "Bring him a fritter."

It was pretty funny that even most *grown-ups* were afraid to get on Cyril's bad side. If her mother had been there, she would have said something like, "Oh, this is ridiculous. Bobby, just come over here and get a fritter." Which would have made her father nervous, but then again, *a lot* of things made her father nervous.

The line Cyril had drawn to show the end of his property was long gone, so Bobby picked up a stick and carefully drew a new one.

"You'd better make sure that it's in *exactly* the right place," Emily said.

Bobby looked worried.

"Just kidding," she said, and handed him his napkin and fritter.

He nodded, but stayed a healthy distance behind the line.

Everyone at the picnic table was still talking about the weather reports, and as the school bus pulled up, she could hear Mr. Washburn saying, "Okay, but they tell us we're getting a huge hurricane at least six times a year, and when was the last time it actually *happened*?"

On the bus, people were talking about the possible hurricane, too, but mostly because they all hoped that a huge storm meant that school would be cancelled for a couple of days. In Maine, though, the weather had to be really bad for the schools to be closed. *Seriously* bad. The power would have to be out *and* the roads would need to be flooded, and maybe some buildings would have to be crushed to bits, too.

Her teachers had apparently all gone, like, hurricane-happy, because every single one of them came up with lessons and assignments using the same general theme. Her social studies teacher gave a lecture about the history of hurricanes in New England, although Emily got pretty drowsy when he started talking about the potential economic impact of a massive storm on a coastal community. Everyone else must have been dozing off, too, because at one point, Mr. Lambert clapped his hands loudly and said, "Come on now, wake up, people!"

Then, during the next period, her English teacher made them all write haikus about hurricanes. Emily was really bad at haikus, but after spending five minutes with her mind coming up completely empty, she ended up writing:

So very windy
Should we all go hide somewhere?
Until it is gone?

"Very nice, Emily, thank you," Ms. Ledoux said, although Emily was pretty sure that she was just being polite. After Karen had read hers, which had "*Dark shadows leaping!*" as the first line, Ms. Ledoux had nodded about ten times and said, "Yes! Very evocative, yes!"

Bobby hated writing and always said he was really bad at it, but everyone in the class laughed when he read his haiku aloud:

Here comes a big storm
Fly, seagulls! Fly for your lives!
Fly, gulls! Save yourselves!

During her science class, her teacher, Mr. Strader, had pulled up a bunch of satellite photos and articles from the Internet, and created a complicated assignment where they were all supposed to plot the path of the hurricane.

For the most part, Emily really didn't know anything about storms, except that meteorologists always got awfully excited and were constantly repeating that it was "a Category 5 storm!" But then, a little while later, they would usually change it to a Category 3 or a tropical storm, or maybe just a tropical depression.

Her science teacher handed out printed-out charts of the Atlantic Ocean and the eastern seaboard, and they spent almost the entire class period tracking the storm's progress, and plotting little points on their papers. Since the hurricane was still somewhere down near Bermuda, there wasn't that much to do, but Mr. Strader was still very enthusiastic, and explained about all of the many differences among tropical depressions, tropical storms, and the various categories of hurricanes and everything.

"Isn't this terrific? It's a *teaching moment*," he said, beaming happily.

For the last fifteen minutes, they were supposed to guess the probable track of the storm, its results, and write a paragraph about why they thought so.

Mikey, who sat behind her, drew his storm so that all of the Mid-Atlantic states were devastated by massive flooding, and Bobby, who sat on her left, directed the storm so far inland that most of the Midwest was destroyed, complete with drawings that looked like little explosions. Not to be topped by that, Scott's drawing resulted in Florida, Georgia, and both Carolinas being permanently uninhabitable, except for packs of roaming wolves.

In fact, most of the people in the room seemed to be competing to see who could draw the most horrible storm, and there was a lot of laughing—especially when people started making the storm go right through, over, and across Maine, leaving nothing but disaster and debris in its wake.

It was funny, but not the kind of thing Emily would enjoy doing herself.

Sitting at the desk to her right, Karen drew a careful curve where the storm gently nudged Cape Hatteras and then blew harmlessly out to sea, leaving nothing but a wisp of a memory behind.

"That's a very sweet hurricane," Emily said.

Karen nodded. "Not even any tree branches blew down."

Emily had to admit that part of her really just wanted to draw a storm that was *attractive.* Balanced, geometric, logical patterns, guiding the eye effortlessly across the page.

"Don't be *boring*," Bobby said, apparently reading her mind.

"I like the eastern seaboard," she said. "I kind of want it to stay in one piece."

He shrugged. "Totally boring," he said, and went back to his own paper.

In the end, Emily created a whirling dervish of a storm, which would smack the coastline briefly, spin out to sea, gather power, and smack the coast again—before running out of steam *completely*, right before it got to Georges Bank, and Casco Bay beyond. No one got hurt, and no buildings or boats were damaged. All in all, she liked her version of the storm very much.

In art class, her teacher, Mr. Reed, asked them

all to "draw the wind," which sent most of the class into an anxious panic.

"Could we just draw breath?" Karen asked.

"Or *break* wind?" Mikey suggested, and everyone laughed.

Mr. Reed fluttered his hands, either to represent wind—or maybe just birds. "Use your imaginations, my friends. I have nothing but faith in you."

People were grumbling uneasily as they held charcoal pencils and looked down at blank sheets of paper, but Emily thought the assignment was pretty excellent. He wanted *motion*, that's all. Energy. Action. Speed.

Cool!

She started sketching so rapidly that everyone in the room was staring at her.

"Well, of course, *Emily* can do it," someone said grumpily. "But what about the rest of us?"

"Just have fun," Mr. Reed said. "You'll all do fine."

Privately, Emily kind of liked being known as the best artist in the class, but she would never say anything like that aloud—even to one of her good friends. So she started sketching more slowly and discreetly—until she forgot and went back to her normal pace.

She drew a tree bending backwards, then a fussy lady with her umbrella inside out, and a little boy who had been blown right up into the air and looked quite startled by the situation. She was in the middle of creating a man whose arm had shot up to try and grab his blown-off hat when she suddenly found herself drawing—for no apparent reason—a window in the middle of the page.

She looked at the partially open window, and the curtains she had started to draw, in complete confusion. Why had she done *that*?

And it had totally wrecked the rest of her drawing, too. The composition of the image made no sense at all now.

"What?" Karen asked, apparently seeing her expression.

Emily picked up her rubber eraser. "I don't know. Artist's block, or—I don't know."

Karen nodded wisely, and went back to drawing curvy lines and arrows pointing in different directions, which was her version of wind, it seemed.

Emily carefully started erasing the window, although she found herself wanting to draw *another* window, and maybe a door, and—it was a specific door. As a matter of fact, it was the back door in her house. So her drawing of a window was a lot less random than she had thought.

Back at home, Zachary must be running around the house, trying to come up with a way to get outside—and come over and visit her.

Apparently, she wasn't just going to be able to read his thoughts now. She was going to be able to *draw* them, too.

Weird. Very weird.

But, also, cool!

10

In the meantime, though, Zachary was trying to leave the house—which she didn't want him to do. She closed her eyes so she could concentrate, and tried to picture where he was at that very moment.

Okay. He was scratching at the door.

She sent him a quick "*Stay!*" instruction, and had the sense of him instantly stopping what he was doing and looking around guiltily. She didn't want his feelings to be hurt, so she thought, "What a good boy!"

With luck, he was wagging his tail.

Then, she imagined his big cushioned dog bed, and him lying down and sleeping blissfully. Within about thirty seconds, she got an image of him sprawling across the couch—which maybe wasn't ideal but was a lot better than him running through the streets to come over to the school.

Which he must have sensed had flickered across

her mind, because she was pretty sure he was scratching at the door again.

So she let herself fully picture the couch, and how comfortable it was, and what a nice place it would be to take a nap.

"Why are you drawing a couch?" Karen asked.

Emily looked down at her paper, where her originally very nice hurricane drawing was getting wrecked all over again. "I, um, seem to be getting static in my head. From"—she didn't want anyone else in class to overhear them, or guess what she was talking about—"you know who."

"We'll have to find some tinfoil and make you a little hat," Karen said cheerfully.

Emily nodded. "We can make you one, too, and then, we'll both be really, really popular."

"We'll look awfully pretty," Karen agreed—and since she was always very optimistic, Emily had a sneaking suspicion that she might be halfway *serious*.

She picked up her eraser again and began erasing the couch, although at this point, the drawing was probably a lost cause. While she was erasing, though, she made a point of picturing the couch again and what a nice, soft place it was to sleep—and hoped that Zack was getting the message.

Just in case he still had other ideas!

It was her father's "early day" at the college, so he picked her up after school. He gave Bobby a ride home, too. They ran a couple of errands on the way home, including a stop at the grocery store.

"Don't forget to buy milk and bread, people!" Bobby shouted, when they went inside. "Protect yourselves!"

Emily laughed, but noticed that just about every single grocery cart *did* have milk and at least two loaves of bread—since that was what Mainers *always* bought to prepare for storms. No one seemed to know why, but everyone did it, anyway. Eggs, too, usually—which didn't make sense, either.

Once, before a rumored ice storm—which had never arrived—Emily had asked her father why he was buying so much bread and milk. He had blinked, thought for a minute, and then said, "Well, because."

She had waited for a better answer, but that was all she got.

Emily, personally, saw absolutely nothing wrong with stocking up on a bunch of snack foods instead, but her parents would usually get healthy stuff like peanut butter and apples and cheese and stuff. If her mother was feeling *really* crazy and bold, she might add a package of blueberry muffins. But Emily could usually talk her father into adding some cookies or candy bars or other fun stuff to their basket—and this time, she got him to let her buy some boxes of very sugary and unhealthy cereal, too.

Once, during a big blizzard a couple of years earlier, her father made a point of fixing them all toast and hot chocolate before the power went out, so that they could say later that, yes, they actually *had* consumed bread and milk while riding out the storm.

It was kind of funny, but a surprising number of people they knew in town had been *impressed* when they heard about it later.

After they dropped Bobby off and went home, Zachary was waiting for them at the door when they arrived.

"Hey there," Emily said, and patted him.

Zack barked and wagged his tail and jumped around a lot. In contrast, Josephine strolled into the kitchen, yawning widely. Emily reached out to pat her, too, and Josephine swished her tail back and forth, but also purred.

It took a few minutes to unload the groceries from the car, with Zachary running around underfoot and getting in the way. Out of curiosity, Emily went into the den and felt the couch cushions—and they were quite warm.

So he had taken her advice and slept there all afternoon. Good for him!

Her father had decided to cook two batches of chili, one with beef, and one that would be vegetarian. He examined recipes in about six different cookbooks, and then began setting out the ingredients he would need.

It was usually a good idea not to interfere when her father was cooking, because he could get pretty intense. He was actually an okay cook, but he always followed recipes *exactly*, and got rattled if any ingredients were missing and he might have to improvise.

So Emily sat quietly at the kitchen table, eating some yoghurt and doing her homework. Josephine had decided to lie right across the pages of her math book, which meant that she could only read the problems by lifting up a stray paw or tail here and there.

"Oh, this is terrible," her father said suddenly.

Emily looked up.

"I can't make this without two more carrots," he said. "And another onion. I need a medium onion. And—" He peered down at two of the cookbooks that were still open in front of him. "Wow, quite a few things, really."

Emily certainly would not mind setting aside her math homework. "Do you want me to go down to Cyril's?"

"Yes," he said, reaching into his wallet for some money. "That would be great, thank you."

It would also be an excuse to walk Zack—and *not* to work on math for a while. "Do you need anything else?" Emily asked.

"Let me check," he said, and scanned the recipes. "We only have dried parsley, not fresh. So that isn't ideal, is it?"

She wasn't a cooking expert, either, but it seemed like it would still probably be okay. "I don't know. But Cyril might have some."

The Mini-Mart was quite small, but even if someone asked for a *really* obscure item, Cyril would almost certainly frown and think for a minute, and then say something like, "Check the third shelf in the fourth aisle, two-thirds of the way down," and more often than not, whatever it was would be sitting in precisely that spot.

She hadn't even gotten up yet, or put her pencil down, but Zack was already standing by the door, wagging his tail with great anticipation.

Her father scribbled out a short, but detailed, list, while Emily put Zack's leash on.

It was pretty cloudy out, but warm, and the air had a nice clean smell of salt and the ocean and evergreen trees. Zachary meandered here and there, sniffing *everything*, and Emily let him take his time.

There were quite a few cars in the Mini-Mart parking lot, and Cyril was doing a landslide business selling—big surprise!—milk and bread. He liked Zack, so she was allowed to bring him inside, as long as she kept him on his leash. No one seemed to mind, and usually people were happy to see him.

Today, a lot of people, including the Henriks and Mrs. Parsons, were standing around near the front counter, watching the latest weather report. The storm must have been powering up, because the weatherman looked downright *gleeful*. Everyone said hello to her and patted Zack—especially Dr. Henrik, who was still very grateful about having been rescued from underneath his car that time.

Right now, the storm—which was now officially called Hurricane Maria—was being described as a probable Category 2 storm, and if it got as far as

Maine, it was being projected to hit land sometime late Friday night.

"I don't know," Cyril said, shaking his head. "I've never seen much of a hurricane, and I've been here longer than *dirt*."

Both of those things were probably true, but Emily wasn't sure if it would be tactful to agree about the dirt part, so she just smiled and nodded.

He frowned at her. "*Dirt*, I say. Longer than the granite that holds this whole coastline *together*."

Okay, that must mean he wanted her to agree. "Yes, sir," Emily said politely. "You're sure right about that."

Cyril nodded, looking somewhat mollified. "Seen plenty of storms come, but mostly, I seen 'em *go*. And this one'll be a *piffle*, compared to Bob and Carol." He folded his arms across his—not small—stomach. "Now, that Bob, *that* was a storm. Lost bridges all over Androscoggin, and all those rich fools, the ones who didn't secure their boats, came back to find a right big mess. I was just a little one during Carol, but that was a *real* storm. Can't say I remember much, mind you, but I surely will never forget it."

Emily couldn't really follow the logic of that last part, but she nodded again. "Yes, sir. I can imagine, sir. The storms up here now aren't nearly as bad."

He nodded again, his expression pleased. "That's sure right, Emily. Are you big enough to remember the ice storm? *That* was some nifty weather. And we had a fine blizzard back in '78. But, this here? Rain and maybe a little wind, I say."

"Gloria wasn't so much," Mrs. Parsons said. "Lost a couple trees, couple boats, is all I remember."

"The marina got hit pretty hard in that one," Bertie Jones, a big, bearded man who worked in the fish market, said.

Ms. Stenhouse, who ran a popular local pottery studio, nodded. "Not as bad as Donna, though. Of course, that was before my time."

"Well, you're from away," Mrs. Parsons said kindly.

"That's true," Ms. Stenhouse conceded.

Emily thought that was pretty funny, since Ms. Stenhouse had lived in Bailey's Cove for more than ten years and really ought to be considered a local by now. But it didn't work that way in Bailey's Cove.

"Well, I don't expect it'll be any kind of fancy hurricane, but there's nothing like a good nor'easter," Cyril said happily. "But I guess it won't be *near* cold enough for that."

"No, sir, it sure won't," Emily said cooperatively.

He smiled at her. "You are a wise young lady, Emily, despite that riffraff you run around with."

Poor Bobby. He hadn't even gotten a chance to *eat* the candy bar he had stolen when he was little, because Cyril had snatched it right back from him before he could take his first bite.

"My dear momma and pop-pop used to talk 'bout the Great Fires of '47," Cyril said. "And my great-great-grandfolks were caught in the Portland Gale, the story goes."

Mrs. Parsons nodded. "We lost some kin when the S.S. *Portland* went down. Terrible, terrible tragedy, that was."

Emily had learned about the famous Gale in school. It had happened back in 1898—and because of the way history seemed to blend all together in New England, it never surprised her that even Mainers who were born one hundred years later were still talking about it.

There was a long, pensive silence in the store.

Dr. Henrik frowned. "You know, think I'll take some duct tape, Cyril. Can't hurt."

Bertie nodded. "Me, too. Might just as well be prepared."

"Me three," Ms. Stenhouse said.

"Me four," Mrs. Washburn, who had just come in to pick up her milk and bread, said.

Cyril always seemed to have *everything* in stock, and he had an entire *section* devoted to tape. Duct tape, electrical tape, masking tape, Scotch tape, double-sided tape—Cyril had them all.

While everyone else was stocking up on tape, Emily checked the list her father had given her. She had already gotten the carrots and onions and dried chipotle peppers, but she still needed to find some of the other ingredients.

"Do you have fresh parsley?" she asked.

"I certainly do," Cyril said, and opened a dairy case, where a huge bunch was arranged in a white plastic container of water. "Fresh from Clara Nordell's garden. But I thought you all were growing parsley in yours, too? I remember when your mother bought the seedlings from me."

Ah, the family garden—which was mostly notable because it had been a complete and total failure all summer, in spite of their best efforts. "Something kind of ate it," Emily said. In fact, animals—maybe deer or raccoons, or even *Zack*—had chewed up almost every single thing that had grown in the garden. As far as she could tell, the only thing they had left behind was the weeds.

"Too bad," he said. "I know your mother was pretty gung-ho, at first." He rolled up a small bunch of the parsley in some waxed paper and then sealed the small package with butcher's tape.

Just then, the front door swung open, and when Emily heard the thump of a cane on the linoleum, she knew it was Mrs. Griswold.

Everyone else in the store immediately stopped talking, although Zack wagged his tail and tugged at the leash, so he could go over and greet her. But Emily held him back, since Mrs. Griswold always said that she didn't like dogs. She could tell he was disappointed, but because he was *the best dog ever*, he sat down next to her, although he kept wagging his tail.

It was absolutely, completely, *painfully* silent in the store.

"Good afternoon, Abigail," Mrs. Henrik said.

Mrs. Griswold nodded a short nod back.

"Hi, Mrs. Griswold," Emily said. "How are you?"

Mrs. Griswold nodded again, although it was maybe slightly less abrupt.

"Well," Mrs. Parsons said, after another long silence passed. "I guess I'll be heading on home now." Then, she looked at Cyril. "Board up those front windows, if you ask me. In case it's *more* than a little rain."

Cyril waved that aside. "It's not going to amount to much." He paused. "But, yeah, I might put up a bit of plywood."

As Cyril rang up Emily's order, Mrs. Griswold limped into line behind her, with a small basket full of milk, bread, two rolls of duct tape, batteries, and some cans of soup, Boston baked beans, and stew.

"Not too concerned about the health code, eh, Cyril?" Mrs. Griswold asked, nodding towards Zack.

Which was kind of unnecessary and mean, in Emily's opinion.

"He behaves a whole lot better than some of my other customers," Cyril said stiffly.

"He sure does," Mrs. Washburn said, and scowled at Mrs. Griswold. "I *never* should have voted for you."

That made no sense at all, but Emily just patted Zack protectively, said a pleasant good-bye to everyone, and then carried her bag of groceries outside. She was about halfway home when she heard the squeak of old bicycle wheels, which could mean only one thing.

Mrs. Griswold was coming towards her!

11

Instinctively, Emily braced herself. Not that she thought Mrs. Griswold would run her over—probably—but she couldn't help feeling a little nervous.

For some reason, Mrs. Griswold never drove, so she either walked very slowly on her cane when she did errands, or she pedaled her rickety ancient bike around town in obvious pain. There was a basket on the bicycle, where she would put grocery bags and other supplies.

It went without saying that, whenever they saw her riding by, Bobby would call her "Miss Gulch" under his breath.

Zack let out a friendly bark when she rode by, but Mrs. Griswold kept pedaling unsteadily past them without a response.

But then, about a hundred feet up the dirt road, she stopped and waited for them to catch up.

Emily didn't want to have a conversation, so she slowed her pace. But Zack was prancing along happily, and it wasn't as though she could let him go off by himself, so she had to follow him.

She didn't feel like talking to her, but it would be too impolite to walk by without a word. "You stocked up on milk and bread?" Emily asked.

Mrs. Griswold's nod was a little wry. "Naturally."

"We did, too," Emily said. "I mean, earlier."

They stood there awkwardly.

"Well, I'd better get this stuff home to my father," Emily said. "He's waiting for me."

"I expect you should, then," Mrs. Griswold said.

The sooner, the better, as far as Emily was concerned.

"That wasn't about you," Mrs. Griswold said after her. "At the store. It was only directed towards Cyril, and I really ought not to have included you in any way."

More to the point, she shouldn't have included *Zack*, no matter what problems she might have with Cyril. Emily rested her hand on Zack's back. "He's *very* well-behaved in stores." Very well-behaved everywhere, in fact.

"Then I guess I owe both of you an apology," Mrs. Griswold said, "don't I?"

Wow, really? *That* was something new. Emily nodded. "Thank you, that's very nice of you."

Mrs. Griswold just shrugged and laboriously mounted her bicycle again. Then, she paused. "You're an oddly graceful child, aren't you?"

Since when? Emily shook her head. "No, I'm actually really clumsy. My father says it's because I'm growing so fast, and can't always find my feet."

Mrs. Griswold smiled a little. "That wasn't what I meant," she said, and then rode away.

Okay, whatever. One of these days, Emily should probably stop being surprised that most of her encounters with Mrs. Griswold were pretty weird.

They were almost home when Zack stopped abruptly in the middle of the road, and she almost fell over him.

"What?" she asked, looking around in confusion. Everything seemed perfectly quiet and normal.

Zack was concentrating so intently that she couldn't get any feel at all for what might be bothering him. He sniffed in one direction and then in another direction and held his paw up indecisively. Then, he must have made up his mind, because he pulled her directly into the woods.

The underbrush was very thick with brambles and dense grass, and there were trees everywhere, too, of course. Zack led her through a small clearing in the woods and towards a big cluster of bushes. As they got closer, she could hear some very loud squawking. *Frightened* squawking.

A bird. Okay. And it was obviously upset.

She could see that it was a seagull, tangled up in a large bush. The bird looked exhausted and frustrated. The more it struggled, the worse the tangle seemed to get.

"Hi," Emily said, for lack of a better idea.

The gull squawked so loudly that she couldn't help flinching.

"Wait, be careful," she said to Zack, who was already using his teeth to rip branches free. "We don't want to hurt it, by accident."

She put her grocery bag down and then lifted a couple of branches, one at a time, to give him an example. Zack seemed confused, but he cooperatively moved more slowly, instead of tearing his way through the bush.

Could she communicate with a seagull? Probably not. But she imagined the bird being calm and quiet, just in case it could read her mind somehow. Then, she reached in through the remaining branches, cautiously putting her hands on the frantic bird, able to feel its heart pounding.

"Shhh," she said. "You'll be just fine." She patted the bird a couple of times, hoping that it wouldn't peck her.

It looked as though one of the bird's feet was caught by some branches, and that its wing was pinned in place by something, too. Thorns, maybe. She eased the bird's foot loose, and it flapped its free wing wildly, trying to escape.

"It's okay," she said, holding the bird's upper body with soothing hands. "Let me do it."

Zack jumped up, and she could see that he was about to dig into a bunch of the thorns with his front paws.

"No!" she said quickly, although that might have sounded too strict. "Zack, I don't want you to get hurt." She quickly imagined his paw caught in the thorns, and he almost instantly backed off. "That's right, good boy," she said.

She had to be very slow and patient, to work the thorns out of the bird's wing, and she managed to prick herself at least twice, but she finally pulled the last of them free. Then, she lifted the bird to safety and held it for a moment, trying to figure out if it was injured. She couldn't see any blood, and as far as she could tell, the gull's wings didn't appear to be damaged.

Now what? She pictured the bird walking a few steps in the clearing, and then flapping its wings experimentally. That way, she could find out for sure if it was okay. With luck, Zack was passing on the message, too.

She set the bird down on the ground on some pine needles, and it shook itself so violently that Zack leaped back out of the way in alarm. The gull took a couple of shaky steps, seeming very unsure of itself. Then, it seemed to gain confidence, and its next steps were much steadier. It stretched its wings all the way out to both sides, and Emily couldn't see any signs of pain or injury.

Now, the gull flapped more aggressively, lifting a couple of feet into the air, hovering briefly, and then fluttering back down. Once it was on the ground, the gull turned its head and looked at them. Even though its little yellow eyes were unblinking, Emily had the sense that it was winking at them and thanking them for helping.

Then, the bird gathered itself and lifted into the air. It flew a few graceful circles around them, cawing triumphantly. Suddenly, several other gulls came flying out of the sky, and glided around the top of the clearing, answering him with welcoming squawks. The gull she and Zack had rescued swooped up to join them, and then the small flock flew off towards the ocean, and out of sight.

"Very cool," Emily said to Zack, and patted him on the head. It was a relief to know that the gull was not only okay, but had also found its family or friends, and could join them again.

Zack was nosing at her hand, and she noticed that she was bleeding slightly from the thorns.

"I'm fine," she said. "I just got caught a little."

He made an anxious sound, and she patted him again.

"Really, I'm fine," she said. "Let's get this stuff home, before Dad starts getting all nervous about his recipe and stuff."

Both versions of her father's chili turned out surprisingly well, and Emily had two helpings of the vegetarian one. He had used two different kinds of mushrooms, for texture, and added some tempeh—which is sort of like tofu—too.

In exchange for her father doing the cooking, her mother cleaned up after dinner. Emily took Zack out to the yard for a few minutes, and then came back in and helped her finish up the dishes.

"Here's something totally weird," Emily said, as she dried one of the pans that didn't fit in the dishwasher. "When I was at Cyril's today, Mrs.

Waldman said something about wishing she hadn't voted for Mrs. Griswold."

Her mother nodded. "When your father and I first moved here, she was the mayor."

Well, that made no sense. Emily lowered the pan. "Wait, I don't get it. You mean, Mrs. Waldman was the mayor?"

Her mother shook her head. "No, Mrs. Griswold was the mayor for fifteen or twenty years, I think. She resigned right after her husband died."

Really? That was hard to imagine. "So, wait," Emily said, still trying to process the whole concept. "She was the mayor"—which meant that she must have been popular once—"and now, no one's *nice* to her?"

"Small towns are strange," her mother said, scrubbing away on a pan.

"That's when Mr. Newell came in, then?" Emily said. Mr. Newell was the current town mayor, and had been for as long as she could remember. He didn't really seem to *do* much, other than appear at various civic events and shake hands, but he was a jolly—and rather round—man.

"No, the deputy mayor was appointed to finish the rest of her term." Her mother frowned. "But that didn't work out very well."

Apparently, there was, like, a whole long story here that she didn't know. Emily tilted her head curiously. "What happened?"

"He, um—well—embezzled," her mother said, looking uncomfortable.

Wow! Small towns really *were* strange. "You mean, he stole?" Emily asked. "From Bailey's Cove?"

Her mother nodded. "He was having some personal problems, and sometimes, people make—bad choices."

Yes, stealing money from the town seemed like a *really* bad choice. But it was suspicious that her mother had only referred to him as "the deputy mayor," instead of mentioning his name. "Do I know him?" Emily asked.

Her mother avoided her eyes. "I don't want to invade his privacy, Emily."

Okay, so, that meant that she *did* know him. Emily thought about that, trying to figure out who it might be. It was probably someone . . . shifty and unpleasant. But she couldn't quite think of anyone who matched that description. "Mr. Thompkins, maybe?" she guessed. He ran a lobster stand that was only open during the summers, and he wasn't shifty, exactly, but he was—gruff, sometimes.

"No, no, not even close." Then, her mother

sighed. "I guess I should tell you, so you don't have to guess. It was Mr. Carter."

Mr. Carter? Their *mailman*? Emily frowned, having trouble putting that together with the friendly man with little gold-rimmed glasses who always carried biscuits in his pockets to give to all of the dogs who lived on his route. "But he's really nice. And everyone likes him."

"Well, after he, um, came home, he's been making a point of paying it all back, a little at a time," her mother said. "And I think everyone appreciates that."

"Came home" must mean— "You mean, he actually went to *prison*?" Emily said, staring at her.

"It was minimum security," her mother said, sounding faintly defensive.

Oh, well, okay. That changed everything. Emily laughed.

"People make mistakes," her mother said. "And this is a very good example of someone trying to move on, and do his best, afterwards."

There was a familiar note in her mother's voice, which meant that she might be able to break into a meaningful discussion. "Is this going to be the part where I learn lessons and grow and everything?" Emily asked.

Her mother nodded. "I'd like to think so, yes—but I'm not getting my hopes up."

That was probably a good idea, yeah. "It's still kind of weird, though," Emily said. "They're all nice to Mr. Carter, who did something really bad, but they're really mean to Mrs. Griswold, who didn't. How come?"

Her mother shrugged, handing her another pan to dry. "Mr. Carter is *friendly* to them, and they just plain like him."

Maybe it was that simple, yeah, but it still seemed wrong.

"Was she a good mayor?" Emily asked.

"Excellent, actually," her mother said. "A little too sure of herself, maybe, but a fine administrator."

Since she was a political science professor, her mother was kind of an expert on government stuff. She'd even worked as a campaign advisor for a few campaigns, including the most recent election for their local state representative, as well as one of their senators.

"Small towns," her mother said again. "They're really strange."

Emily nodded. It seemed as though *that* might be the only answer which made any sense.

* * *

The front-page headline in the *Bailey's Cove Courier* the next morning was "Batten Down the Hatches! Historic Hurricane Heading North!" "Oh, *definitely*," her mother said, just as her father was saying, "Maybe we should leave town."

In any case, the storm had been upgraded from a hurricane watch to an official hurricane *warning*. Emily assumed that if the storm became a genuine hurricane that hit land, they would all be able to figure out that part for themselves.

Her father decided that after work, they should go out and buy emergency "go" bags, as a precaution. He also planned to stock up on candles and batteries, make sure all the cell phones were charged, and fill up plastic containers with fresh water—just in case.

As they sat at the breakfast table, her father looked thoughtfully at the window over the sink. "Think we should tape all of the windows?"

"I guess it would be safer," her mother said. "But it won't be much fun cleaning off all of that adhesive later."

"It'll be a nice birthday chore for Emily," her father said cheerfully.

Emily knew he was kidding, but immediately

pictured herself standing on a rickety ladder, scrubbing glass and sighing a lot.

Zack looked up at her anxiously, and she realized that he didn't like the idea of her being at the top of a ladder by herself. So she pictured herself standing on the ground, holding a long pole with a sponge attached to the end of it—and that must have made him feel better, because he settled down again.

"Your mother and I can go out to supper tonight, and maybe a movie," her father said, "and won't it be nice for us to find the job finished when we get home!"

Not everyone got her father's sense of humor, but she thought he was pretty funny. Wacky, sometimes, but funny.

However, if they were voting, her choice—just in case—would be *not* to tape up the windows.

Emily helped herself to another English muffin. "I think it's a really good idea for me to stand up on the biggest ladder I can find, with tape and all. Maybe I'll even stay home from school and get an early start."

Her father nodded. "We could hire you out to the neighbors, too. Might be a good way to pick up some spare cash."

The rest of breakfast was just general silliness, while she and her father tried to top each other with zany and impractical financial plans. Zachary seemed to enjoy the tone in their voices, because he kept wagging his tail the whole time, although Emily had no sense that he was paying close attention to the conversation. Her mother had also tuned out and was highlighting and taking notes about something in an academic article she was reading.

Finally, though, her mother looked at her watch. "Emily, you have about nine minutes to make your bus."

Cyril's was a six-minute walk, so she had better get moving. But, by the time she had brushed her teeth, she was cutting it *really* close and had to run the last hundred yards to jump on the bus before it pulled away.

By that afternoon, Bailey's Cove was now officially at "Inland Hurricane Watch" status. The weather people kept changing their minds about the storm, though. First, they would say it was going to be a Category 2 storm; then, they would decide it was going to be a whopper of a Category 4; and then, an hour later, they would suddenly be describing it as "heavy rains with some high winds."

Her mother had called Bobby's mother to

arrange for her to walk home with him from the bus stop. Most of Bobby's family were going to be down at the boatyard doing storm preparations, and Bobby wanted to go there, too, and secure his own boat. After being assured that they would be properly—and extensively—supervised, Emily's mother agreed that she could join him, and that either she or Emily's father would pick her up at about five thirty.

On the way, they stopped at Emily's house, so that she could get Zack and feed Josephine.

"Hey, I'm going to put these in your garage," Bobby said, pointing at a set of lawn furniture. "You guys shouldn't leave anything like that outside, with the storm coming."

"Are you actually worried about it?" Emily asked curiously.

Bobby nodded, already hauling a chair across the grass. "Yeah. I mean, you know, what if *bread* got scarce?"

Okay, so he was kidding. "You're kidding, right?" she asked, just to be sure.

He grinned at her. "Well, yeah, about the bread." Then, he frowned. "But maybe not about the rest of it."

Everyone had been so busy being hardy New

Englanders that she had forgotten to consider the possibility that a dangerous storm could genuinely be about to hit Bailey's Cove. "So, you think this storm is the real deal?" she asked.

Bobby thought about that, and then nodded very seriously. "Yeah," he said. "I think it's going to be *huge*."

For the sake of the town—and the entire state, for that matter—Emily hoped that he was wrong.

But she was starting to suspect that he might not be.

12

When they got down to the boatyard, the place was the most active she had ever seen it—even more than the day the annual lobster boat races were held. There were people everywhere driving forklifts, small tractors, flatbed trucks, and trailers hooked up to cars. Fishermen, workmen, the harbormaster, Coast Guard members—no matter where she looked, it was crowded and noisy, with people yelling instructions and giving directions.

The air was also filled with the sounds of various machines and motors and power tools, and people were carrying ropes and tools and waterproof coverings and rubber hoses and ground anchors and all sorts of other supplies. Others were topping off fuel tanks, checking bilge pumps and generators, attaching fenders, and removing electrical equipment, sails, and any loose equipment from their boats. She saw some unfamiliar people with special instruments and gauges, taking mysterious measurements, and she heard someone saying they were from organizations like FEMA and the National Weather Bureau.

There were even some reporters and photographers, watching all of the activity and filming it for evening newscasts and Internet websites.

"Wow," she said.

Bobby nodded. "Last night, everyone at the pound"—meaning his parents' lobster pound—"was sitting there debating about what to do. Like, if they should haul out, or just secure everything, or what."

As far as Emily knew, when it came to storms, it all pretty much came down to who made the best-educated guesses—or who was just plain lucky. Some people thought their boats would actually be safer in the water, heavily anchored and covered and tied down. Other people would decide to go to the extra work of hauling their boats out of the water, up the steep cement driveway, and onto the shore. Then, in most cases, they would be strapped down, protected with special shrink-wrapped plastic coverings, and secured by ropes or bungee cords. Very cautious boat owners might even drive their boats—safely resting upon their trailers—miles away from the shore and any possible damage from the ocean.

Since it was still only September, a lot of the

people who owned vacation homes in the area were still coming up for occasional weekends to sail or fish. So not many of them had hauled their boats out for the season yet. A few of them had been able to come up to Maine to supervise the process or had hired local workers to do the job for them, but apparently, some of the owners hadn't even *called* the boatyard yet, so the harbormaster and town official were trying to decide what they should do to protect their boats. It was kind of a tough situation, because if they made the *wrong* decision, and someone's boat was damaged, the person would be really upset. On the other hand, if Emily owned a really expensive boat, she figured she would probably keep an eye on local weather reports every day and check in regularly.

"What's everyone in your family going to do?" Emily asked.

Bobby shrugged. "I don't know. Still making up their minds. Dad's just going to secure his boat, but Cousin Eddie's going to haul his out. Aunt Martha wants to leave hers in, but figures she has to set a good example, for the rest of the collective"—she was the president of the Bailey's Cove fishing collective—"so, she's trying to figure out the best way to go."

As far as Emily could tell, it looked like most of the smaller boats were being brought ashore, while the larger ones were being secured with lots of long mooring lines and anchors, and would be left in the water to ride out the storm. Some of the boats were being anchored close to the docks, while others were going to remain out in the cove. The boating supplies shop up near the harbormaster's office was doing a landslide business, as people bought extra plastic coverings, tarps, nylon ropes, thick straps, floats and fenders, precut lengths of galvanized chain, anchor and dock lines, sheets of plywood, rubber hoses—which were used as chafing gear to help protect the boats if they bumped into the dock or something—and lots of other supplies. Plus, of course, the shop was selling dozens of rolls of *tape*, especially duct tape.

Bobby waved at his father and brother, who were down by the edge of the cove, with their cousin Kate's regular sternman, Seth. The three of them were carefully guiding a beautiful big sloop out of the water. Once they had hauled it up on shore, it would be mounted onto a boat rack, strapped down, and carefully blocked into place to protect it as much as possible from the storm.

"Some of them are paying, like, a couple hundred dollars each to take care of their boats," Bobby said. "Maybe even more. Larry's going to get *rich*."

Emily nodded. The boat owners who lived far away weren't likely to have any trouble finding locals to hire, since a lot of them would be really happy to earn the extra money. No wonder there were so many eager volunteers milling around all over the place!

But what if the storm didn't hit at all? Would the boat owners be upset that their boats had been hauled out of the water for no reason—or would they figure better safe than sorry?

Zachary must not have liked the sense of chaos, because he sat down in some sand and panted for a minute.

Emily patted him. "It's okay, buddy. They're just making sure the boats will all be safe."

He wagged his tail, but still seemed edgy. Since animals were able to sense bad weather, she wondered if he could already tell that a big storm was coming.

"It'll be okay," she said reassuringly, and filled a small tin bowl with fresh water for him to drink.

Bobby was going to secure his boat safely inside the family storage shed. Aunt Martha and Seth came over to help them lift the frame off its sawhorses and onto the tarpaulin Bobby had spread out across the cement floor.

"It *will* be safe here, right?" he asked, for about the tenth time.

Aunt Martha nodded. "It should be, Bobb-o. I mean, there's no way to predict how bad the storm is really going to be, but unless there's a massive storm surge, or it turns into a Category 5, it should be pretty well protected in here."

Bobby looked uneasy, but nodded.

Aunt Martha spread some plastic sheeting over the frame and then strapped a nylon line across it. She connected each end to metal hooks that had been mounted in the flooring as ground anchors.

"Do it just like that," she said. "Use as many straps as you can, and then you can secure it in place. But don't connect them to anything that isn't sturdy."

Bobby nodded, already reaching for another piece of nylon rope. "When we're finished, we'll put plastic and stuff on everything else in here, too. And move stuff off the shelves and all."

"Good bet, Bobby. Let us know if you need

anything else, okay?" Aunt Martha said. "We'd better go out and help herd the cats."

Emily laughed, since the chaos outside did seem like a bunch of stubborn and unruly cats running around like crazy.

Bobby nodded. "Thanks, Aunt Martha. Thanks, Seth."

The upside-down frame had been put on top of the unfinished parts of the boat, and then covered with a blue tarpaulin. After using several pieces of rope, she and Bobby also stretched some sturdy bungee cords across the frame, attaching the ends to pipes and metal hooks and anything else in the shed that seemed really strong.

When they were finished, Bobby checked and rechecked the connections, and pushed on the frame in several places, to make sure that it was firmly in place. Then, his double-checking turned into *triple*-checking, and Emily started to feel really sleepy. She looked over and caught Zachary yawning—and couldn't help wondering which of them was actually the sleepy one.

Then, Zachary stood very straight—and Emily automatically straightened up, too, without knowing why she was doing it.

"What?" she asked.

She couldn't see anything wrong, but Zack was on full alert. Maybe it was just because there were seagulls screeching and swooping down to snatch up bits of bait and fish?

But now, she heard a metal grinding sound, which she couldn't locate—except that Zack was already bolting off in that direction. Without thinking about it, she took off after him.

"Hey, where are you guys going?" Bobby asked, and then joined in the chase.

Zack was making a beeline towards the water, and Emily was *really* hoping that they weren't going to have to jump in. Then, she saw that a metal cable holding a large motor boat had frayed badly and was about to—wait, it *had* snapped!

"Hey, look out!" she yelled, as the boat started rolling down the steep cement slope.

But the fisherman standing below the boat didn't even turn around, and she could see that he was listening to an MP3 player and bobbing his head in time to the music.

Zack leaped in the air, hit the guy chest high, and sent him flying backwards.

"Hey, what are you doing, dude?" the guy protested. Then, he saw the boat hurtling towards him. "Whoa!" he shouted, and rolled out of the way.

Emily wasn't sure if Zack was going to be safe, so she dove onto *him*, and then Bobby landed on top of *both* of them. All three of them ended up in a big pile, as the boat careened past them before crashing loudly into a wooden pylon with a distinct crunch of fiberglass.

Other people were running over to help, but the boat had already come to a stop, and luckily, none of them had gotten hurt. The fiberglass hull was pretty badly damaged on one side, and the rudder was also smashed up.

"Oops," the fisherman said quietly.

"Probably should have just left it in the water, Joe," someone said.

The fisherman nodded wryly. "*Now* you tell me." Then, he smiled at Zack, Emily, and Bobby. "Thanks. That was a close one."

Very close.

Her parents arrived at the boatyard to pick her up a little while later. People were still buzzing about Zachary's amazing rescue, and her parents uneasily accepted congratulations.

"That all sounds rather risky," her mother said, as they got into the car. "Was it?"

"Risky" was a hard word to define. "I think it

probably *looked* pretty dramatic," Emily said. Which wasn't a lie, even though it didn't precisely answer the question she had been asked.

"Hmmm" was all her mother said in response.

Buying supplies for emergency knapsacks involved going to a bunch of different sporting goods and hardware stores, since lots of places had sold out of most of their survival gear. They ended up driving down to L.L.Bean in Freeport, Maine—which was always fun—to get all of the items they couldn't find closer to home.

They bought three knapsacks—one for each of them. Emily also picked out a small red duffel bag, which was going to be packed with everything Zack and Josephine might need for a few days, if they all got evacuated.

The best part of the shopping trip was that they stopped to eat at a really good Mexican restaurant on the way home.

Her mother had gone to a bunch of websites, downloaded relevant material, and printed it out, so they were following the Maine Emergency Management Agency's suggestions pretty much to the letter. Ultimately, her parents had decided not to go buy sheets of plywood and nail them over the windows, since the shutters would probably suffice.

Her father had fastened most of them shut that afternoon, so the house looked a little bit strange and unfriendly to Emily. While he had been doing that, her mother had stored her kayak, Emily's bicycle, some deck furniture, and some other things safely inside the garage.

It took over an hour for them to unwrap all of their purchases and pack up the knapsacks and duffel bag. There was a battery-operated weather radio called an "NOAA," an old-fashioned can opener, paper cups and plates, plastic silverware, some canned food, juice boxes, flashlights, lots of batteries, first-aid supplies like Band-Aids and aspirin and hand sanitizer, toothbrushes and toothpaste, small pillows, clean underwear, socks, and t-shirts, three light fleece blankets, disposable plastic rain ponchos, plenty of empty Ziploc bags, pens, pencils, notepads, a deck of cards, and a few paperback books. Her mother put together some small plastic bags of lightweight snacks like granola bars, raisins, crackers, and peanut butter. She also tucked an envelope of cash into each of the knapsacks, since the electric power was likely to go out, and that meant that ATM machines wouldn't work.

Emily took responsibility for packing up the duffel bag for Zachary and Josephine. She also brought Josephine's cat carrier downstairs and put it near the back door. She packed up some of the disposable fresh water packs they had bought at one of the camping gear stores, plus cans of food, plastic dishes, a pack of cat treats, a Ziploc bag full of dog biscuits, Zachary's pain medication, a disposable cardboard litter box, and two thick towels.

"If we have to go to a shelter, we're supposed to have copies of their vaccination records to get in," she said.

"Well, that's technically true," her mother agreed. "But I don't think it will be a problem because everybody *knows* us."

Okay, yeah, that was a good point.

For that matter, there was a decent chance that someone who worked at the animal hospital—maybe even their vet!—would be evacuated to the same shelter, if the storm got bad.

The knapsacks were pretty full now, although each of them kept putting in little extras, like a hairbrush, sunglasses, a book of crossword puzzles, her father's never-used Swiss Army knife, an extra cell phone, and that sort of thing. Emily had charged up her iPod, too, so she would be able to listen to music.

And they also packed up three small rolls of—duct tape!

13

Right before bedtime, the telephone rang. It was Emily's grandparents, who reported that the airline had told them that flights into Maine for the next couple of days were all going to be canceled, and the airports in New York were already closed or had very long flight delays. So that meant that they wouldn't be able to come up for Emily's birthday, which was really disappointing, although not much of a surprise, with the storm looming.

"We'll do it next weekend, and you'll get an *extra* celebration, Ladybug," her grandfather promised on the telephone.

Emily had absolutely no idea why he called her "Ladybug," but she liked it—as long as no one she knew at school found out.

"Can we all go on the trail ride next weekend?" she asked her grandmother, when it was her turn to talk to her.

Her grandmother laughed. "I'm sorry, love you

dearly, Emily—but, no, not a chance. I'm just not a horsewoman."

Well, the whale-watching cruise was still a good alternate plan.

After they had hung up, Emily saw her mother sitting at the kitchen table, looking very uncertain.

"What's wrong?" she asked.

"Since your birthday is on the weekend, am I supposed to make cupcakes and bring them to school tomorrow?" her mother asked uneasily.

If her mother, who had actually once *been* in junior high, didn't know the answer, she sure didn't, either. Emily shrugged. "I have no idea."

"Oh," her mother said, and thought that over. "Maybe I had better call Aunt Gail, and see what she thinks."

When in doubt on parenting issues, which happened sort of often, her mother invariably consulted books—and her various siblings and in-laws—*at length*, before making up her mind.

So Emily decided to rescue her. "I think junior high is probably too old. The ninth graders would laugh at me."

Her mother nodded, clearly relieved. "Yes, I think you're right."

"Of course, you could bake a bunch of cupcakes anyway, just for us to have," Emily said.

"How about I promise to make cinnamon French toast tomorrow morning for breakfast?" her mother suggested.

Hearing that, her father came in from the den. "What, and *deplete* our milk and bread?"

Her mother smiled. "I think we would still have enough left to survive, Theo."

"Whew. I don't mind baking cupcakes, if you want," he said.

"And deplete our flour and eggs?" Emily's mother asked. "And—perish the thought—the *sugar*?"

"Yes, let's be very, very bold," her father said, and then looked at Emily. "Want to help?"

"If you let me deplete the frosting bowl, when we're done," she said.

"That's a deal," he promised.

The next morning was blustery. The skies were cloudy, and it was raining. When Emily looked out her bedroom window, she could see that the ocean looked grey, but not particularly threatening.

Zack, however, seemed a little antsy, and she wondered if he could sense that the storm was going to hit soon.

"What do you think?" she asked him, as she got ready for school.

But she couldn't really get a good feel for what he was thinking; just a sense of general anxiety.

Emily bent down so she could give him a hug. "It's going to be okay. Even if it hits, everyone's ready, and it won't last that long."

Zack wagged his tail, but in a distracted sort of way, and she still could feel strong anxiety coming from him.

"Don't worry, it really will be all right," she promised.

Josephine was asleep on the bed, so *she* certainly didn't seem very worried—which was comforting, as far as Emily was concerned.

Downstairs, her mother was, indeed, making cinnamon French toast, while her father went outside and fastened the last few window shutters.

"Does he need help?" Emily asked.

Her mother used a spatula to flip two slices in the cast-iron frying pan. "No, he's almost finished. Better safe than sorry, right?"

Absolutely. But it was strange to have the house seem so dark—and a little spooky—with the shutters closed.

In addition to French toast, the kitchen smelled like coffee and bacon, and even though she would never dream of eating any, she had to admit that it sometimes smelled pretty good. Or maybe it was just Zack who wanted some?

"Is it okay if Zachary has a piece of bacon?" she asked.

"Of course," her mother said, and flipped one in his direction.

Zack caught the crisp slice easily, and ate it with obvious delight.

Her mother had tuned the radio to the local station, and Emily was hoping to hear an announcement that school had been canceled, but so far, everything from day-care centers to yoga classes to the weekly bingo tournament seemed to be open as scheduled. The meteorologist was concentrating on the marine forecast, with small- and large-craft advisories, predictions of very high seas, wind gusts of at least sixty or seventy miles an hour expected, possible storm surges, and gale warnings in effect. Every so often, he said cheerful things like, "Well, now, we seem to have quite a bit of chop out on the bay this morning!"

Mostly, though, it just *looked* like a storm was

coming—without much of anything actually happening, other than some rain—and Mainers were too tough to stay home for that.

"Maybe I should miss school today," Emily said experimentally. "Keep an eye on things."

"Nice try," her mother said, and poured her some more orange juice.

"Or as a pre-birthday reward?" Emily said.

Her mother shook her head firmly, and Emily looked at her father—who had just come inside—and he also shook his head.

Well, it had been worth the effort, at least.

When Emily headed out for the bus, her parents were filling a few more plastic containers with fresh water, just in case. Opening the windows a tiny bit was supposed to be a good way to equalize the pressure during a hurricane, and maybe keep the glass from shattering, and she was pretty sure they were going to do that, too.

The hurricane had been downgraded to a Category 2 storm, instead of a Category 4, for now, and was supposed to hit full force sometime late that night or maybe very early Saturday morning. But a few of the local meteorologists still thought it might just blow back out to sea and never really hit land, and everyone at Cyril's was nodding a lot, and saying, "See? We *never* have hurricanes in Maine." Or, anyway, almost never.

But, if the storm was bad offshore, a lot of people all over town were going to be really worried about friends and family members who were out on long fishing trips. Some of the ship captains might already be heading back, but since the fishermen and women needed to catch enough fish to be able to pay their bills, a lot of the boats would probably stay out as long as possible and just try to ride out the storm. There were all kinds of limits and rules about where people could fish and how much they could legally catch, and that made it really hard for people like Bobby's family to make a living.

Bobby called on her cell phone while she was waiting on the bus to let her know that his parents were letting him stay home from school, so he could help them with some last-minute storm preparations. She was pretty envious that he didn't have to go, but most of her other friends would be at school, since they lived in Brunswick or other inland areas and didn't have to worry about coastal storms in the same way that people in Bailey's Cove did.

So it was just a normal school day. They had a pop quiz in math, played volleyball in gym class, and split up into groups of four to have stilted conversations in Spanish. Mostly, they just asked each other how old they were and if they felt well, since those were the only two topics where they all actually knew the correct words to use.

By eleven, it was pouring outside, and so windy that the trees on the playground were whipping around, and little torn-off branches kept smacking against the classroom windows. Things like trash cans and stray red rubber kickballs were blowing around all over the place, too.

By eleven thirty, Mrs. Wilkins, the principal, came on the intercom and announced that school was going to be dismissed early, and the buses would be waiting outside to start taking students home as soon as they had gone to their lockers and gotten their coats and everything.

Emily wasn't the only one who hustled, since they all wanted to be safely on the buses and on their way home before Mrs. Wilkins had a chance to change her mind and tell them all to come back inside.

Emily was about halfway home—texting with Karen, who was on a different bus—when her phone rang. She glanced at the number and saw that it was her mother, so she picked up right away instead of finishing her current text message.

"Hi," she said cheerfully. "What's going on?"

"Hi. They put out an email telling us they were dismissing all of you early," her mother said.

Emily still didn't get why parents and teachers were always so *nervous*—or why the schools sent out mass emails constantly, about everything from the possibility of catching the flu to bake sale announcements to constantly updated scores of the soccer game at the sixth-grade picnic the year before. "Yeah," she said. "I was about to call you and let you know."

Except that, okay, maybe she had kind of forgotten. Oops.

"I have a class starting in about five minutes," her mother said, "but why don't I let them know I'm going to be late, and run over right now and pick you up?"

Double oops. "I'm on the bus," Emily said.

"What bus?" her mother asked.

That seemed like kind of a goofy question. Did her mother think she had maybe headed down to the Portland bus terminal to leave town? "I'm not sure, but it's really crowded and I think it's going to

Montreal," Emily said. "And I've never been there, and the ticket wasn't very expensive, and I thought it would be cool, so I just, you know, *got on*."

There was a long silence on the other end.

"You're not supposed to start being snarky until you turn thirteen," her mother said.

Emily grinned. "I guess I'm, like, *advanced*."

"Mmm," her mother said, sounding a little annoyed, but also amused. "Well, why don't I call Bobby's mother, and maybe you can go home with him and stay there until your father or I can come get you."

"Bobby didn't come to school," Emily said. "They had him stay home to help with the boats and the lobster pound and all."

"Oh. Okay. Well, maybe you can go over to the Peabodys, or—" Her mother stopped. "They're still in Florida, aren't they?"

As far as she knew. "I'll go and hang out with Mrs. Griswold," Emily said, and then laughed.

Except her mother didn't join in. Was she maybe *considering* that as a possibility?

"I don't suppose she would care for that," her mother said finally.

Not hardly, no. "It's not a big deal," Emily said. "I'll just go home and wait for you there."

"Why don't you wait at Cyril's, instead," her mother suggested. "I'll be there as soon as I can."

Instead of answering, Emily repressed a long-suffering sigh, since she would much rather just go home and play with Zack and Josephine.

"Emily, I have a class full of students waiting for me," her mother said. "Do you promise to go to Cyril's?"

Emily nodded, even though this entire conversation was making her feel like a five-year-old. "Okay."

"And please send me a text right away, letting me know that you're there," her mother said.

Now, she felt more like a *two*-year-old. But she agreed, and once they had hung up, she went back to texting with Karen—during which she complained a fair amount about her parents being way too strict.

When the bus stopped at the end of the dirt road, she politely said thank you to Mrs. O'Toole, who—as usual—just grunted, or maybe said, "*Meh*"—she couldn't tell which. She had expected to see the regular group of people hanging out at the Mini-Mart, but to her surprise, the parking lot was empty, the store was closed, and the front windows were boarded up with plywood.

Surely, her mother couldn't expect her to sit here and wait when it was completely deserted, right?

The weather was worse than she had expected it to be. The wind had picked up even more, so that it was almost hard to walk. The clouds were very thick, and such a dark and threatening grey that if she had been, say, *ten*, instead of less than a day from turning twelve, she might have been scared. It was also raining so hard that she was completely soaked before she'd even walked twenty feet, and there were already knee-deep puddles everywhere.

The water out in the sound looked *fierce*, with big grey waves and whitecaps, and carefully secured boats already thrashing against their ropes. She could smell fresh sap everywhere as branches snapped off trees, and the dirt road was littered with fresh leaves.

Luckily, since she *was* almost twelve, none of it bothered her at all. But it was starting to rain even harder—and *that* was the only reason she decided to run the rest of the way to her house.

The wind was so strong that she had a little trouble pulling the back door open, and it whooshed around the kitchen before she got it closed again. Zack and Josephine both ran to meet her, and she gave each of them a big hug.

“Don’t worry,” she said. “It’s only a storm. Everything’s okay.”

She hoped so, anyway.

Even with the shutters closed, the windows seemed to be rattling, which was creepy. It seemed as though she could hear the rain inside the house, but finally she figured out that it was coming down the chimney. She couldn’t really think of a solution to that, so she just put a couple of plastic tubs in the fireplace to catch the water, and stuffed two old beach towels in there, too.

Then, she remembered that she was supposed to let her mother know that she was waiting safely at Cyril’s. She couldn’t seem to get a signal on her cell phone in the kitchen, so she walked around, holding it up in the air, hoping that she’d be able to pick something up. But, even in their attic, she wasn’t getting any sort of signal at all, so maybe the cell phone tower in their area was broken or something?

Well, that was no problem, since they still had a landline. She hurried back downstairs, with Zack and Josephine trailing right behind her. Their nervousness was making her feel edgy, but she tried to ignore the sensation. Instead of waiting for her parents to get home, maybe she should just call

Bobby's house and ask one of his parents to come over and pick her up.

She picked up the receiver in the kitchen, but there was no dial tone. She tried hanging it up and dialing again—but there was still no response, no matter how many different buttons she pushed.

Maybe a telephone pole had fallen down, too? The wind seemed to be getting stronger with every passing minute, and she heard lots of branches crashing down to the ground outside.

Her computer had a wireless connection, so maybe she could send out email? It was probably connected to their phone service, of course, and wouldn't work, but it was still worth a try.

But on her way upstairs, suddenly, all of the lights went out! That meant that they had just lost their power, too. Now she didn't have electricity *or* phone service—or any way of calling for help.

There was no question in her mind that the hurricane was here now—and she was all by herself!

14

Okay, she didn't want to panic. Well, no, she *did* want to panic, but that wasn't going to help much. Maybe the Henriks were home, and she should try walking up to their house? But, if they weren't home, she would have risked going out in the storm for no good reason, and would have to make her way back here through the wind and—no, that was a bad plan. And Bobby's family lived quite a bit farther away, so that wouldn't work, either.

Even though the windows were shuttered, she would need to find a place to sit that was away from any potential broken glass. She looked around the dark house uneasily, and decided to drag a kitchen chair over to a windowless alcove at the base of the stairs.

Then, for lack of a better idea, she sat down. Josephine instantly curled up on her lap, although "huddled" might have been a better word. Zack was too big to get onto the chair with them, but he managed it somehow, and Emily moved to one side to try and make room for him.

"It's going to be fine," she said, hoping that her voice sounded very confident. "Mom and Dad will get here soon, and—it's just a little rain, that's all."

The animals snuggled closer, and the only sense she got from either of them was that they were frightened.

When she first heard the bullhorn outside, she wasn't sure what it was. There was a loud mechanical voice yelling something about "Please evacuate immediately!" She didn't know what to do, and she couldn't see outside through the shuttered windows. But, while she was trying to make up her mind, there was a loud knocking on the door.

"Hello?" a voice called. "Police department! Is anyone home?"

She definitely wanted to open the door, but she had been taught long ago *never* to open the door to strangers when her parents weren't there.

However, Zack was wagging his tail, and she could see a faint flicker of red and blue lights outside. So, it probably *was* the police, and someone she knew.

"Hello?" the voice shouted again.

Zack barked twice.

"Hey, Zack," the voice said, and Emily was almost sure that she now recognized the person's voice, and that it was Officer Jarvis, who she knew. "Is anyone home?"

"Officer Jarvis?" Emily called back cautiously.

"Yes, Emily, it's me," he said. "I'm here with Officer Taylor. Can you open the door, please? We need for you all to evacuate right away."

"Hi, Emily," Officer Taylor said. "The hurricane's looking more serious than we expected, so we're evacuating the whole neighborhood."

Hearing her voice, too, Emily decided that it was okay, and she opened the door—which took a lot of effort against the wind.

Both police officers were wearing foul weather gear, but still looked very wet from the rain.

"Where are your parents?" Officer Taylor asked. She was fairly tall, with dark blond hair, and was a member of her mother's kayaking club, so Emily knew her pretty well.

"I don't know," Emily said nervously. "I mean, still over at the college, or on their way home, or—I'm not sure. The phones aren't working, or the power, or anything."

"Well, we're evacuating this entire part of town over to the VFW Hall," Officer Jarvis said. He was stocky, with brown hair and a neatly trimmed mustache. Because he owned horses and rode all the time, he had been assigned as the only member of the department to do mounted patrols. But of course, today, he and Officer Taylor were in one of the town's regular squad cars. "Why don't you write them a quick note, so they'll know where to find you?"

Emily nodded, scribbling a fast explanation of where she was going, and then put the note in the middle of the kitchen table, so her parents would be sure to see it. "I need to bring Zack and my cat, Josephine, with us," she said.

Both police officers nodded—which was a relief, because if they had said she couldn't bring her pets, she would have refused to go.

Josephine had gotten scared, and at first, Emily couldn't find her. She tried to hurry, but Josephine wasn't hiding in any of her usual places. She usually hid whenever she saw the cat carrier, anyway, but the storm had made her even more jittery than she would normally have been.

"I'm sure the cat will be fine, Emily," Officer Jarvis said, after a few more minutes had passed. "We can just take you and Zack over. But we really need to go right now, before the roads get any worse."

There was *no way* Emily was going to leave her cat behind. "Zachary," she said quietly, just to be sure she had his attention. Then, she pictured her cat as clearly as possible. "Where's Josephine? Go get Josephine."

Zack wagged his tail and ran into the den.

Emily had already looked in there, but she trusted him to know exactly where to go. So she followed him with the cat carrier, and saw that Josephine was hiding in the corner behind one of her father's file cabinets. It was a challenge to catch her, but then Zack put his paw out and held Josephine firmly in place. Emily quickly scooped her up, guided her into the cat carrier, and fastened the door shut.

"Okay, good," Officer Jarvis said, looking relieved. "Come on, let's hurry."

Her parents had lined up all of their emergency supplies right near the back door, and Emily was glad that they had planned ahead. The go bags were pretty heavy, so she just grabbed her own knapsack, and Zack and Josephine's duffel. Presumably, her parents would come and get theirs before they came over to the shelter.

They all dashed outside through the sheets of rain and headed straight for the squad car. Officer

Taylor put the bags in the trunk for her, while Emily arranged Josephine's cat carrier on the backseat. Then, Zachary jumped in after her.

Officer Jarvis was talking to someone on his handheld radio, although the connection was full of static and hard to understand. "Will do," he said finally. "Jarvis out." Then, he glanced at his partner. "The whole peninsula's been evacuated now, except for—well, you know."

Officer Taylor groaned. "I can guess," she said.

Emily could, too, and her guess was right, because they drove straight to Mrs. Griswold's house. Officer Jarvis got out of the car, while Officer Taylor announced the evacuation order over the bullhorn. Mrs. Griswold must have heard it, because she opened her front door before either police officer had even made it up onto the porch.

"I'm sorry to bother you, ma'am," Officer Jarvis said. "But we're under orders to evacuate the area."

Mrs. Griswold shook her head. "That's all well and good, but I don't follow orders. You all just move along now."

That was exactly the way Emily would have expected her to react, but she couldn't help wishing that Mrs. Griswold would cooperate for once and not make things so difficult for people.

"Mrs. Griswold, I'm sorry, but I really must insist," Officer Jarvis said.

She scowled at him. "You can insist all you like, Mortimer, but this is my home, and I'm not going anywhere."

Mortimer? Gosh. Emily had never known that his first name was *Mortimer*.

Officer Taylor sighed. "Mrs. Griswold, this isn't coming from us—it's an official government evacuation order. So, we need for you—"

"I am in possession of all of my faculties, and I'm allowed to make my own decisions. My choice is to stay at home," Mrs. Griswold said. "And now, I really think it's past time for you to take this child, and her pets, to a safe location."

Emily thought the two officers might argue some more, but then there was a loud cracking sound as a big branch snapped off a tree and fell onto the road.

"All right, then," Mrs. Griswold said. "I'm going to go inside now, instead of standing out here in the middle of this mess like a fool. Do your jobs, and take Emily over to the storm shelter."

With that, she limped back up onto her porch, went inside, and slammed and locked the door.

Just then, *another* huge branch came crashing down across Mrs. Griswold's driveway.

"All right, come on," Officer Taylor said urgently. "Let's get out of here before it gets any worse."

It was strange to sit in the backseat of a police car, and Emily was surprised to see that there weren't any handles on the inside doors. Officer Jarvis was talking on the radio, and it sounded as though everyone else in town who lived in potentially dangerous areas had already been safely evacuated.

Josephine was complaining to herself inside her carrier, but Zachary was sitting up alertly on the backseat and seemed to think that the whole thing was an excellent adventure. Of course, it was also possible that he was just happy to be riding in a car, which was one of his all-time favorite things to do.

"Do you think Mrs. Griswold will be all right?" Emily asked. "Is she breaking the law?"

Unexpectedly, Officer Taylor laughed. "It's not ideal, but no, it's probably not against the law in *Maine.* People are mighty stubborn here. Besides, that house has stood through an awful lot of storms, and I imagine it will probably still be right there when this one's over."

Emily immediately imagined Dorothy's house being picked up in the twister in *The Wizard of*

Oz—the notion of which seemed to *horrify* Zack, whose ears went down.

"Sorry," she said softly, and pictured the house sitting safely and securely on its foundation, instead.

It was raining so hard now that the windshield wipers didn't make much difference, and some of the wind gusts were so powerful that it felt as though they were shaking the car. Since Officers Taylor and Jarvis were visibly tense, Emily didn't say anything and just patted Zack and kept an eye on Josephine inside her cat carrier.

Luckily, the VFW Hall wasn't very far away, but the drive was still pretty scary. Officer Taylor had to swerve out of the way of falling branches and airborne objects more than once, and the rain kept pounding on the roof of the car.

They had to stop and pick up Mr. and Mrs. Brody and their parrot, Hortense, because their SUV had gone into a ditch. Officer Jarvis called the incident in, but they didn't stay to see if they could do anything about the car, since the storm was getting stronger every minute.

The backseat was very crowded now, and Zack was half on the floor and half on her lap, while she held Josephine's carrier on her lap, too. Hortense must have been nervous, because she kept repeating the same two phrases—"The Yankees stink!" and "I want candy!"—over and over.

When they got to the VFW Hall, there were a *bunch* of cars and pickup trucks parked out front. People were hurrying inside with bags and bundles and knapsacks and supplies, ducking their heads to try and avoid the fierce rain and wind.

The building must have had its own generator, because she could see the low golden glow of lights inside. The VFW—which was the abbreviation for the Veterans of Foreign Wars—Hall had been built on Bailey's Cove's version of high ground, which pretty much only meant that it wasn't actually on the coast, and that the building was on top of a tiny hill. Also, the brick walls were thick and sturdy, and there were only two small windows in the front, and the building probably wouldn't blow down no matter *how* powerful the hurricane was.

Probably.

Officer Taylor had explained on the way over that the town was planning to set up cots inside the hall, and serve sandwiches and coffee and stuff like that from a small kitchen area. If it got too crowded, the Ping-Pong and air hockey tables were going to be moved out of the cramped basement, but the pool table was so heavy that it would have to stay down there.

Emily was very curious to see what the VFW was like, because she had never been inside before. She knew that local veterans held meetings and charity fund-raisers there sometimes, but other than that, it had always been sort of mysterious to her. So it was sort of disappointing to see a lot of card tables and folding chairs and other perfectly ordinary furniture. There was also a large American flag mounted on one of the walls.

Cyril, who was the president of the local VFW chapter, laughed when he saw her expression. "Did you expect something more interesting, Emily?"

Yes. "Well, I guess I maybe thought it would be a little bit more *decorated*," Emily said.

Cyril laughed.

"So, there aren't any secret rituals or anything?" she asked.

"Mostly, we just play poker," he said.

Well, then, that explained the vast number of card tables.

She looked around and saw that Bobby and his entire family had pretty much taken over the back right corner of the hall. There was a snack table set up on one side of the room, with soda and juice and bags of chips and pretzels, and what appeared to be plates of homemade cookies. People were setting up cots and sleeping bags and getting everything organized. The room was already very crowded and noisy, and it looked as though every single person from this part of town was here.

Except for two very important people.

Her parents.

Where *were* they?

15

Bobby waved her over, and she went to sit with him and his family. She set Josephine's cat carrier down on the floor, and Zack made himself comfortable on the floor in front of her folding chair.

"I don't see your mother and father, Emily," Bobby's mother said.

Emily nodded. "I know, I'm not sure where they are. They might still be at work?" Except she knew that that wasn't at all likely. "I left them a note at the house."

"I'm sure they're fine," Bobby's mother said, patting her hand reassuringly. "Mostly, I expect that they're just worried about *you*."

That was definitely true, and the roads were so awful that they were probably having to drive really slowly and carefully, too.

"Don't worry about a thing, Em," Bobby's father said heartily. "They'll walk through that door any time now."

But they didn't. The storm was getting stronger, and her parents were *out* there somewhere. People like Cyril were insisting that they were probably just sensibly staying in the house and waiting until the storm passed—but Emily knew them better than that. A note wouldn't be enough. They always worried so much about her that they would need to see for themselves that she was safe.

People kept hurrying into the building—wet and disheveled and carrying supplies—and she looked up eagerly every time the front door swung open.

But it was always someone else, not her parents. And it had been a *really* long time now. More than enough time for them to have gotten home from work and come over to the shelter. Enough time for them to have done it more than once!

"Can you please go look for them?" she asked Officer Taylor at one point.

Officer Taylor shook her head reluctantly. "I'm sorry, Emily, it isn't safe. And other than going to the house, we wouldn't even know where to *start*."

"They're smart people," Bobby's uncle said. "*Professors.* They'll know better than to be wandering around in the middle of this."

"Well, they *are* from away," someone said in a low voice—and everyone else in the room glared.

"They're fine, Emily," Bobby's mother said. "I can understand why you're worried, but I'm sure they're fine."

Emily nodded, but felt her hands clenching into tight, nervous fists.

It sounded like there were big *explosions* going on outside—with violent, cracking sounds—and she could see people in the dimly lit room cringing every time it happened.

"What is that sound?" Bobby whispered.

Emily shrugged nervously. "I'm not sure."

"Trees," Bobby's father said, looking a little grim.

"Are they *blowing up*?" Bobby asked.

His father nodded. "More or less."

Emily wrapped her arms around herself and felt Zack stir restlessly at her feet. He lifted his paw and put it in her hand, and she held it for a minute.

"Good boy," she said automatically, and his tail thumped on the floor.

She could tell that Cyril was watching her, and he suddenly got up and went over to Officers Taylor and Jarvis.

"Why don't we just send out a small search party?" he suggested.

Officer Jarvis shook his head. "I'm sorry, but it's much too dangerous. We can't allow that."

"We have a room full of military veterans here," Cyril said. "Do you think maybe we don't *know* a few things about danger?"

Officer Jarvis nodded respectfully. "Yes, sir, I know you do. But if anyone goes out in the storm, it's going to be *me* and my partner, and we can't risk it for a wild-goose chase."

"What if we just go over to the house?" Mr. Washburn said. "That seems like the most logical place."

Outside, there was another vicious cracking sound, followed by a massive crash, as another large tree must have fallen down.

"*No*," Officer Taylor said. "Instead of two missing people, we would end up with half a dozen missing people. I'm very sorry, but the answer is *no*."

Everyone seemed to be looking at Cyril to see what to do next.

"All right," Cyril said. "For *now*. But, as soon as it lets up even a little, we're going out there." He pointed his finger at Officer Jarvis. "And don't call me sir, Mortimer. I was a *sergeant*."

"Yes, s—" Officer Jarvis stopped. "Yes, Sergeant," he corrected himself.

Emily didn't want them to wait—but she didn't

want anyone to go outside and get hurt, either. What if her parents needed help, though?

Bobby nudged her arm. "My mother's sure that they're just bunked down at the house, waiting. It's going to be okay."

Emily didn't believe that, but she nodded.

Zack was staring at her, and she looked back, thinking as hard as she could about her parents. Zack instantly got to his feet and cocked his head, waiting for her to let him know what she wanted him to do.

"Does he know where they are?" Bobby asked.

"I don't know," Emily said. "But I'm pretty sure he could *find* them." She closed her eyes and pictured her parents again. This time, she imagined them in their house, in the alcove near the stairs.

Zack paced a little, in front of her chair, but she couldn't read what he was thinking at all.

So she pictured them in the car, instead, driving down a muddy road with torrential rain and howling winds all around them—and Zack stood stock-still. The only image she got back was her parents in the storm, but she couldn't tell where it was. Rain and trees, no recognizable landmarks. She couldn't even see a *road*.

"Can you find Mom and Dad?" she asked him. "Do you know where they are?"

Zack looked right at her, and what she saw in her mind was him running through the storm, bounding effortlessly over debris. She also felt strong confidence coming from him. *Extreme* confidence.

Okay. It was horribly risky, but it was the only thing to do. She trusted him to know what he was doing, and to be able to take care of himself.

"He knows, doesn't he?" Bobby said.

Emily nodded, opening her knapsack. "I think so, yeah."

"Are we going to go with him?" he asked.

Emily took out a piece of paper, a pen, a Ziploc bag, and—what else?—her roll of duct tape. "You *know* they'll never let us. But I can say that he *really* needs to go out, and they might let us open the door for a minute."

"And he'll go look for them," Bobby said.

She sure hoped so. She wrote: *Mom and Dad, I'm at the VFW Hall. I'm fine. Stay someplace safe!* Then, she sealed the note inside the bag. "Do you have your Cub Scout knife?" she asked.

Bobby nodded and dug it out of his jeans pocket.

Emily used it to cut off a piece of duct tape, and then fastened the plastic bag securely to Zack's collar.

"Okay, good boy," she said, and then unsnapped his leash and hugged him as tightly as she could. "Go find Mom and Dad, okay?"

Zack licked her face and then charged over to the door.

Emily followed him over and started to open it.

"Whoa there," Officer Jarvis said, putting his hand up. "What do you think you're doing?"

"He, um, needs to go out," Emily said.

Officer Jarvis looked at her suspiciously.

Okay, she was going to have to tell him the truth. "I want to send him to go find my parents," she said.

Officer Jarvis shook his head. "No, not with the storm like this."

"They're my *parents*," she said. "And Zack can find them."

Officer Jarvis hesitated. "It won't be safe for him, Emily. Are you sure you want to take that chance?"

No. "They're my *parents*," she said again.

Zack reared up on his hind legs and scratched at the door with his front paws.

Officer Jarvis looked uneasy, but he nodded. "Okay," he said, and—with Cyril's help—tugged the door open.

Gusts of wind and torrents of rain rushed into

the room. But Zack raced outside—a white streak, disappearing into the darkness. Emily watched him go, swallowing hard. It took several people to force the door closed again, and she *hated* that Zack was now out there, too.

But what choice had she had?

And now, all she could do was wait.

Each minute that passed felt like a century. The wind howled, the rain thundered down, and sometimes, it felt as though the building itself was going to fall apart. Emily held Josephine's carrier on her lap, wishing that she could take her cat out—but she would almost certainly run off and hide, which would only make things worse.

So she just waited.

And waited.

And waited.

Every now and then, she had the blurry sense of rushing through the storm, but as far as she could tell, Zack was so busy concentrating that he didn't have time to try and send any sort of messages to her.

So she kept waiting.

And waiting some more.

"Anything?" Bobby would ask in a low voice, every so often, and Emily would shake her head.

Hours might have gone by—or maybe just minutes. She couldn't tell, either way. But sometimes, she felt cold and wet, or as though she had just stumbled. She also felt *tired*.

Then, out of nowhere, she felt an unexpected surge of relief. She couldn't quite pin it down, but she was almost sure that they were somewhere nearby.

"I think they're outside," she said.

Bobby must have dozed off, because he had to wake himself up. "What? Where?"

"Someplace close," she said. "Really close."

Obviously, she couldn't tell everyone that she was reading her dog's mind, but she got up and went over towards the door.

"I think I hear Zack barking," she said.

Everyone strained to listen, but then, all over the room, she saw people shaking their heads.

"They're out there," she insisted. "I can hear him." Which, okay, she *couldn't*, but that was a minor point, in this situation.

Bobby nodded. "Hey, yeah! I can hear him, too! I think they're, um—" He glanced at Emily for clarification.

"In the parking lot," she said. "That's where I hear him."

"Yup," Bobby agreed. "Me, too."

People were looking at them dubiously, and no one was ready to open up the door yet.

But then, a minute or two later, there were three loud knocks on the door.

Someone was definitely outside!

16

Cyril moved more quickly than anyone else and threw the door open, despite the power of the wind.

To Emily's joy, her mother and father—and Zack!—came stumbling into the room. Her father was leaning on her mother and limping, and they were all soaking wet, but they were *safe*.

Everyone was talking at once, but Emily just concentrated on hugging her parents, and then hugging her dog. It turned out that a tree had fallen on their car! Their airbags had deployed, so they were okay, except that her father had hurt his ankle, trying to stamp on the brakes.

There weren't any doctors in the shelter, but their vet, Dr. Kasanofsky, was there with his family. There was plenty of first-aid gear, and after her parents changed into dry clothes, he strapped up her father's ankle with an Ace bandage. He and Officer Taylor—who had been a paramedic, before she joined the police department—both thought that it might actually be broken.

"Well, *ow*," her father said. "I guess that's why it hurts so much. Can I have two aspirin, please?"

Dr. Kasanofsky gave him some aspirin, and her father swallowed them with hot coffee. He and her mother were both still shivering from being outside in the storm and were sipping coffee to help warm up again.

"You really shouldn't have been driving during this, of course," Mrs. Parsons said kindly. "But that's an easy mistake to make when you're from away."

"Out of curiosity," Emily's mother said, "will there ever be a time when we *aren't* considered 'from away'?"

All of the locals in the room pondered that question.

"If Emily stays in town, and her children have children, *they* would probably count as natives," Officer Jarvis said finally.

Everyone else nodded in general agreement.

All Emily could think was "Wow, tough crowd!"

Despite his ankle, her father was pretty cheerful, and it was nice to sit on cots, eat sandwiches, and take it easy. The storm was howling wildly, and the door and windows rattled sometimes; but it was safe and cozy inside, and everyone was in a good mood.

The truth was, as long as no one got hurt, New Englanders *liked* storms. Crashing waves and rain and wild wind—they probably could have written their own version of "My Favorite Things" about various forms of bad weather.

It was bizarre, but she could hear the church bells ringing at the Methodist and Congregational churches nearby. Clanging and pealing, over and over.

"No one's in the bell towers, right?" she asked.

"Just the wind," Bobby's aunt Martha said.

"Wonder if the boats are okay," Bobby's brother, Larry, said—some version of which other people in the room also remarked every few minutes.

Kurt, who worked on Bobby's father's boat, shrugged. "Not much we can do. No one thought the storm was going to be *this* big. We'll have to wait and see what's left tomorrow."

Josephine was complaining inside her carrier, and Emily took her into a small storeroom, so that she could let her out for a few minutes. She also set up the disposable litter box from the animals' duffel bag, which Josephine immediately, and gratefully, used. After that, she got back into her carrier with no fuss at all.

Emily's father was stretched out on a cot with his ankle propped up, reading with a flashlight, and her mother was sitting at the closest card table playing poker. Emily was happy to sit down, share a cheese sandwich with Zack and Josephine, and drink some orange juice.

But, she did still have one nagging worry, although there wasn't anything that she could do about it.

Was Mrs. Griswold okay?

It was a long night. At one point, it got very quiet outside, and Emily thought the storm must finally be over. But it turned out that it was only the eye of the hurricane, and after about half an hour, the wind was howling more than ever. The windows in the front rattled wildly, and even though Emily knew she was safe and out of range, she couldn't help ducking whenever an especially strong gust hit.

To distract themselves, she and Bobby went over to the snack table, and each of them filled a paper plate with chips and brownies and chocolate cookies. Officer Jarvis was also at the table, fixing himself a ham sandwich.

"Um, sir?" she asked.

He looked up.

"What if, um, Mrs. Griswold isn't safe?" she asked.

"Don't worry, Emily," he said. "That old house has stood through many a storm, and she was born and raised here—she knows what to do."

Probably, but Emily couldn't help feeling concerned, anyway. "Should someone check on her, though?"

He nodded. "You bet. We'll definitely go over there at some point tomorrow and see how she's doing. Unfortunately, we can only *advise* people to evacuate. We can't force them to do it."

"What if she changed her mind?" Emily asked.

He shrugged. "Well, she knows where we are. If she's had second thoughts, I assume she'll show up in the morning."

"No way she'd have come here and have to hang out with everyone all night," Bobby said, as the two of them walked back to the area where their parents were. "It'd be totally awkward, you know?"

Maybe he was right, and that's why she decided to stay home. That would be really sad, because it would mean that she would rather endanger herself than be in a room with all of them.

She and Bobby played Go Fish, and then War for a while, until they were both yawning.

"I'm going to crash," he said.

Emily nodded. She was pretty tired herself.

A lot of people in the hall were already asleep, including her father. Her mother seemed to be wide awake—and had a *really* big pile of poker chips in front of her at the card table.

Josephine was napping peacefully in her carrier, but Zachary seemed to be very uncomfortable and kept rubbing his ear with his front paw. Emily could feel *intense* pressure and pain in her own ears, and Zack's hearing was so much more sensitive than hers that the wind must really be hurting him.

Dr. Kasanofsky had been walking around, checking on people's pets, and when he heard Zack whimper, he hurried right over.

"Is it the wind?" Emily asked. "Or, I don't know, the barometric pressure or something?"

Dr. K. nodded. "I'm afraid so. There's not much we can do to make him feel better, but if you keep patting him, it should help. And if you brought his painkillers along, I think it would be okay to give him one."

Those were easy doctor's orders to follow, and

Emily opened the duffel bag to take out Zack's medication.

Dr. K. checked Josephine, too—who was very annoyed to have been awakened, and hissed at him a few times.

"I think I'll go give Hortense some candy," Dr. K. said, and headed towards the Brodys' parrot, who was still chattering nonstop.

Emily spread a sleeping bag out on the floor, so that Zachary could curl up next to her. Then, she patted him until he fell asleep—which made her so tired that *she* fell asleep, too.

When she woke up, it was still raining, but the storm seemed to be ebbing away. She could hear the wind, but it sounded more like a normal windy day than a storm. It must have been almost dawn, because she could see a faint light coming in through the narrow front windows.

Except for some snoring here and there, the big hall was quiet. People were asleep on cots, in sleeping bags, or sitting up in chairs, and a few people were just lying on the floor, using folded-up coats as makeshift pillows. In fact, she seemed to be the only one in the room who was awake.

She got up as quietly as possible and put on her sneakers. It was kind of chilly, so she pulled on a hoodie, too. Then, she tiptoed to the hall to go brush her teeth. When she came out, Zack was standing there, waiting for her.

"Hi," she whispered, and patted his head.

Zack rested his muzzle on her arm, staring deeply into her eyes.

"What?" she asked.

He trotted down the hall, and for the first time, she realized that the VFW had a back exit.

Well, it made sense that he wanted to go out—it had been a long time for him to wait. She opened the door and followed him outside. The rain was coming down pretty hard, and she raised her hood. There were branches and fallen trees all over the place, with so much torn vegetation strewn around that it looked almost prehistoric. She even saw a tree on top of someone's pickup truck, and it seemed like they were going to have to clear away a lot of stuff before anyone was going to be able to drive on the road, in either direction. All of the nearby buildings seemed to be standing, although the steeple at the Methodist church looked a little crooked.

She expected Zack to come right back, but instead, he ran to the edge of the parking lot. Then, he turned and looked at her.

"Come on," she said. "Let's go back inside and get something to eat."

Normally, breakfast would be his top priority, but he stayed where he was.

"I'm not sure what you—" She stopped, as a vivid image of Mrs. Griswold came into her mind. Mrs. Griswold on the floor, or maybe the ground, somewhere. "Oh, okay. Let's go wake people up, and we can—"

Before she finished her sentence, he was already dashing into the woods. Without giving it much thought, she went after him. If they hurried, they could probably be back before anyone even noticed that they had gone.

The cloud cover was so heavy that it almost seemed dark outside, and the driving rain made it easy to get disoriented. So many trees had blown down—or snapped in half—that she couldn't quite figure out where she was, most of the time. Bushes had been completely uprooted, and things like trash cans and lawn furniture were in strange and unexpected places. Everything just looked too different.

So she just held on to Zack's collar and let him guide her through the tangle of broken branches and splintered trees. The storm drains and the little stream that wandered through the woods both must have flooded, because sometimes, they were wading through at least a foot of water.

The water was up to her knees in most places, and she kept tripping and falling over rocks and logs and other stuff. Maybe coming out here hadn't been such a good idea, after all, but Zack seemed to be very determined. The wind was still so strong that she hung on to tree branches for extra support as they made their way along.

After a few more minutes of struggling through the damaged trees, she could feel mud and gravel under her feet, and figured that they must be on the road now. It was *weird* not to be able to tell exactly where she was—even though they were on her own street.

Her mind must have seemed panicky, because she felt as though Zack was making a point of sending her *calm* thoughts. His pace was steady and sure, and she decided that she would simply trust that he knew what he was doing—and that he would keep her safe. She could see the ocean now, and when she wiped some of the rain out of her eyes, she could tell that they were definitely on her street—which made her feel a lot better. The ocean was as choppy and rough as she had ever seen it, and looked as though it was much deeper than usual. She couldn't see the usual private docks and assumed they were underwater. There were at least two wrecked boats floating on their sides out in the water, even though they still seemed to be connected to their mooring lines.

They got to where she was almost sure Mrs. Griswold's house should be, but it seemed to be *gone*.

She couldn't help gasping. "Zack, it blew away!"

He just kept steering her forward, and as they got closer, she realized that a tree had fallen across the road and crushed the fence, so that the yard was completely blocked. On top of that, the big old oak tree, which had stood near the rose garden, had crashed onto the house and seemed to have crushed the porch and the entire front section of the house. As she got closer, she saw a large window, which would have seemed perfectly normal—if it hadn't been broken and lying in the middle of Mrs. Griswold's garden. One of the other front windows was shattered, and the wooden frame had broken off partially and was swinging crazily in the wind. She could hear scary banging noises, which seemed to be window shutters smashing back and forth against the side of the house at unexpected moments.

She stared, in horror, at the wreckage. Could Mrs. Griswold possibly be okay, if she was *in* there? And if she *wasn't* okay, Emily was afraid to go inside and see that.

She closed her eyes and pictured herself back at the VFW, safely on her sleeping bag, feeling warm and comfortable and *dry*.

Zack must have gotten that message, because he stopped walking and she felt a flash of uncertainty and confusion. But then, he shook some of the water off his drenched fur and began striding forward again.

Okay, so that was apparently a big "no, we're not going to go back there yet" from him.

As they crossed through what was left of the front yard, Zack began to move more cautiously. He would take a step, hesitate, and then step again. Emily wasn't sure why, but she mimicked his movements.

They were on the porch now, and he kept leaning against her legs, pushing her in a distinct direction each time. Emily assumed there must be holes, or weak places, in the porch floor, and he was trying to keep her away from them. There were so many leaves and small branches covering everything, that half the time, it was hard to tell where her feet *were*.

Most of the fallen oak tree was lying right where

the front door had been, so there didn't seem to be any normal way to get inside.

"Mrs. Griswold? Hello?" she called. "Mrs. Griswold, are you in there?"

Of course, with the wind and rain—and the crashing sounds of ocean waves in the background—she could barely hear her *own* voice, forget anyone else's.

"Mrs. Griswold?" she called, more loudly. "Are you okay?"

There was no answer.

She really wanted to go back to the VFW, but Zack was still leading her across the remains of the front porch. The tree was blocking the front of the house, but she could see that most of the door frame, wall, and front window had all been torn away, and that the roof was damaged, too. Zack guided her inside, through the hole in the house, and she squinted to try and see in the dim light. There was lots of water on the floor and furniture was strewn about, but it seemed to be rain and wind damage, not actual flooding.

"Hello?" she called again, trying not to sound as afraid as she felt.

Then she gasped.

There was a body on the floor!

17

At first, Emily was going to run away, but then she saw that the person was, in fact, Mrs. Griswold, and that she was moving one of her arms a little. So she was alive, at least. She was lying on the floor, underneath what appeared to be a heavy mahogany china cabinet, or maybe a bookcase or something. It looked like she was trapped from the waist down.

"Is someone there? Who is it?" Mrs. Griswold said, her voice shaking. "What do you want?"

Okay, so they were *both* scared. "Mrs. Griswold, it's me, Emily," Emily said. "With Zack. We came to see if you were okay."

"Where are your parents?" Mrs. Griswold asked, sounding cross now. "And what are you doing out in the middle of this storm, you foolish child?"

Wasn't the answer to that question obvious? "Well, I'm trying to help *you*," Emily said. "Are you okay?"

From the sound of Mrs. Griswold's sigh, she probably thought *that* question was too obvious.

"I took a spill," Mrs. Griswold said finally.

"Should we try to lift it off you?" Emily asked.

"No, absolutely not," Mrs. Griswold said. "It's much too heavy. But, if you could go and get some help, I would"—she coughed—"really appreciate it."

Okay. That sounded like a good plan. "We'll go right now," Emily said. "The roads are a big mess, but I think they can get here with four-wheel drive, probably. We'll send someone back as quickly as we can."

But, as she turned to leave, Zack blocked her way. She lost her balance on the wet floor and landed on a pile of soaked books.

"Zack, come on, don't do that," she said impatiently.

Zack used his front paw to push her gently down again—and when she tried to sit up, he did it a third time.

Seemed like the dog version of saying, "*Stay.*"

"Zack—," she started, but then had the clear vision of him galloping through the woods by himself, without her.

Without her.

Great.

"Okay," she said. "Good dog. Find Mom and Dad, or—I don't know—Cyril or someone."

Zachary barked once and then leaped over the couch and out of the house—and was gone.

She didn't want to stay behind, since it was wet and dark and scary, and she was stuck in here with a really cranky lady. Also, what if no one understood and knew enough to come back with him? But he could move a lot more quickly than she could, and probably much more safely, too. Besides, even if no one else understood, Bobby would figure it out and get people to follow him and find her.

Mrs. Griswold let out an annoyed breath. "For goodness' sakes, you were supposed to go *with* him."

Yep. That definitely would have been better, as far as she was concerned. Emily shrugged. "He can go a lot faster without me, and—it'll save time."

"If I didn't know better, I'd say that you and that dog read each other's minds," Mrs. Griswold said, sounding very testy.

Emily wasn't going to touch *that* one with a ten-foot pole. "He's just really smart." She stood up, and set the coffee table on its feet, then picked up a rocking chair, too. "I'm not going to try and move you, but should I go into the kitchen and find you something to eat, maybe?"

"No, I have no idea how much damage there is out there, and I don't want you to take a risk and go look," Mrs. Griswold said. "Stay here where it's safe."

Relatively safe, anyway. Emily sat down in the rocking chair, listening to the wind and rain and slamming shutters.

"Um, does it hurt?" Emily asked.

"Well, now, what do you *think*?" Mrs. Griswold snapped.

She thought that it probably hurt a lot, and that Mrs. Griswold might even have a broken hip or something. "I'm really sorry that it fell on you, but the mayor should set a better example," Emily said stiffly.

Mrs. Griswold let out an impatient sigh. "What are you going on about now?"

"It's mandatory to evacuate," Emily said. "And the police asked you very politely, and you *should* have."

"Ah, I see," Mrs. Griswold said. "And I'm sure your parents will be thrilled to find out that you've been out gallivanting in the storm, instead of staying in the shelter—after *your* mandatory evacuation."

Maybe, but it wasn't quite the same thing. "Yeah, well, if you decide to run next November, I don't think you're going to win," Emily said.

Surprisingly, Mrs. Griswold chuckled. "Yes, that's a safe bet, child."

Then, Emily thought of something. "Did you not want to go to the shelter, because it would be so totally crowded and full of people you don't like much"—Bobby's theory—"or did you kind of not care if your house fell down right on top of you?"

She must have gone too far, because there was no response.

"A little of both, I expect," Mrs. Griswold said finally. "But you never heard me say that."

Okay. Fair enough. Being able to keep secrets mattered a lot, as far as Emily was concerned.

But that was a very sad secret.

"Your parents got a bright one, when they got you," Mrs. Griswold said.

With luck, yeah. "I asked my mother one time if she would have minded, if I hadn't been smart, and she said that"—Emily automatically quoted her—" 'the goal of a parent is to maximize their child's potential.' "

Mrs. Griswold laughed again. "If that doesn't

sound exactly like Joanne Feingold, I don't know what *would*."

Yeah, her mother could be a little bit of a professor, sometimes.

"Of course, it wasn't exactly a surprise," Mrs. Griswold said. "After all, your parents knew the mother."

Yeah, fine, whatever. It wasn't as though—*whoa*. Wait a minute. "What?" Emily asked. "What do you mean?"

There was a noticeable silence. A long and *excruciating* silence.

"Just babbling, I expect," Mrs. Griswold said, her voice a little defensive. "Don't pay me any mind."

No way, not a chance. "I don't understand. You're saying that my parents *knew* my mother?" Emily said. There was absolutely *no way* that could be true. Her parents would never keep a secret like that from her. "How could they have? It was a closed adoption."

Mrs. Griswold nodded. "Right you are. It was a long time ago. I'd forgotten the details."

Maybe.

Or maybe not.

Because if they knew her mother, that meant

that a lot of things she had always assumed—and been told—about the adoption weren't true.

That they had been lying to her.

And that wasn't something she wanted to hear from *Mrs. Griswold*, of all people.

Except she knew her parents would never do that. They would *always* tell her the truth. It wasn't as though they were pals with Mrs. Griswold and would have been telling her private secrets or anything like that. Maybe Mrs. Griswold hadn't been quite as mean in those days, but Emily couldn't imagine that she had been a *friend* of theirs.

"It's been a long night, Emily," Mrs. Griswold said briskly, "and I'm running a fever, and I'm very tired. I just made a mistake, that's all. Forget I said anything."

Emily nodded, since she would *happily* forget that they had ever had this conversation. Sure, she might ask her parents later on, but she knew that they would say that Mrs. Griswold was just being weird, and that she had been totally wrong, and that the only sensible thing to do was to be very polite, but also ignore her.

Just then, there was the sound of a couple of four-wheel-drive cars outside, followed by a familiar bark.

Zack came leaping into the house, wagging his tail, and Emily patted him.

"Good boy!" she said. "You're such a good dog!"

Zack wagged his tail even harder, and Emily wished that she had a biscuit or some other treat for a reward. But, for now, a hug would have to do.

The police came tramping into the house, along with two EMTs and Cyril and Dr. Henrik—and her mother. Emily was afraid that she was going to get in trouble for leaving the VFW without permission, so she just stood quietly to one side with Zack, while Mrs. Griswold was put onto a stretcher and eased to the ambulance waiting outside. It turned out that the roads were clear enough to make it to Brunswick, where the hospital was using emergency power from its generator, and Emily's father had already been taken over there to have his ankle X-rayed.

Emily glanced over at her too-quiet mother. "Are you mad at me?"

Her mother let out her breath. "Well, you ran outside without telling anyone, at the crack of dawn, and who knows *what* could have happened?"

That was all true. "I'm sorry. Zack needed to go out, and when he took off, I followed him," Emily said. "I really wasn't thinking about the rest of all that."

"And the two of you rescued an injured elderly person," her mother said.

Yes. But that was a good thing, right?

"Let's go out and get into Cyril's car, so he can take us over to meet your father. I just have one thing to say to you first," her mother said.

Emily waited, nervously.

Her mother grinned. "Happy birthday," she said.

Oh. Right! She had completely forgotten!

When they got over to the hospital, it turned out that her father had, in fact, broken his ankle. He already had a cast and crutches, and was surprisingly cheerful. The early reports were that Mrs. Griswold had a cracked pelvis. A few other people had been brought in with various bumps and bruises, but it didn't seem as though there had been any really serious injuries during the storm—which was very good news.

Cyril dropped them off at the college, where her mother's car was still in the parking lot. When the tree had fallen on their other car on the access road the night before, they had been driving together in her father's Subaru.

They went to the VFW Hall first to pick up Josephine, where Bobby's sister, Andrea, had been keeping an eye on her, until they could come get her. There were a few people left in the hall, cleaning up, but most of the people had already gone.

"Thank you for taking care of her for me. Where's Bobby?" Emily asked.

"Everyone went down to the boatyard," Andrea said. "We heard there was a lot of damage there. I'm hoping everything's okay, though. I'm going to head over there in a little while." She smiled. "And happy birthday, Emily! You're really old!"

Yes. She kept forgetting. Emily smiled back. "Thanks."

Once they were all in the car, they decided that they would go to the boatyard first, and then home. A tow truck had already hauled her father's car off to the service station to be repaired, although they didn't know whether it would be able to be fixed.

"I'm sorry about the car," Emily said.

Her father shrugged. "I'm glad that we're all okay. A car is just a car."

That was definitely true. There were lots of reports of storm damage, up and down the coast of Maine, but as far as she could tell, they were all lucky that it hadn't been even worse. They weren't going to get their power back for a few days, probably, but they would just have to work around that.

"I'm sorry, Emily, but when we get home, I have a feeling your ice cream cake isn't going to be in very good shape," her mother said.

"We can eat it with spoons," her father said.

Emily nodded. "Absolutely. It'll taste just as good."

"It's not really going to be the traditional birthday," her mother said, "but I think we can still have fun."

Her father turned to smile at her. "What would you like that we can actually *do*?"

The mood in the car was nice and relaxed, and Emily didn't want to change that. She was curious enough to *want* to ask them about what Mrs. Griswold seemed to have been saying about her birth mother, but it wasn't as though any of it would turn out to be *true*. So there was no reason to worry about it. From now on, though, she was really going to have to make a point of avoiding Mrs. Griswold even more than usual.

They drove around a curve in the road, and for the first time since the storm, she saw the boatyard. Or, anyway, what was *left* of it. Everywhere she looked, there were broken boats, splintered boards, pieces of fiberglass, fallen trees, scattered rope and barrels and spools of wire and fishing line—and then, Emily saw that Bobby's family's shed had been *flattened.*

Right where his boat had been.

"Oh, wow," Emily said. "Oh, no."

Her mother quickly parked the car, and Emily jumped out, with Zack behind her.

"I have to go help him," she said.

The whole boatyard was filled with wreckage. Some of the boats looked fine, while others were severely damaged. It seemed as though the winds and rain had swirled around randomly, destroying some things and leaving the rest mostly untouched.

People were all over the place, gathering up some of the wood and fiberglass and metal that was strewn everywhere. There were coils of rope, crushed lobster traps, torn sails and tarps, and lots of other trash and debris that was too damaged even to identify. But the storm was gone, and the cleanup had begun.

As Emily got closer, she could see that the shed was nothing but a massive pile of wood and sheet metal and other debris. Bobby was standing there in horror, while his mother patted him on the shoulder. His father and brother were already carrying broken pieces over to a nearby Dumpster.

"Wow. This is awful, Bobby. I'm really sorry," Emily said.

"I can't believe the *boat's* gone," Bobby said miserably.

"Can we help you clean up?" Emily's mother asked.

Bobby's mother nodded, and they all worked together in silence. Emily's father couldn't do much because of his crutches, but he sat at a picnic table and sorted through tools and other small items that people had piled there. Zachary seemed to be trying to help, too, although that just meant that he ran back and forth, letting out encouraging barks.

The sun had come out, and everyone was pitching in, all over the boatyard, trying to help everyone else. There wasn't much conversation, because people were too busy concentrating on what they were doing. When the remains of the shed—and Bobby's boat—had been cleared away, she and Bobby stood there alone for a minute.

"Well, that's that, I guess," he said, with no expression on his face. "I guess it was fun while it lasted."

Emily stared at him. "We aren't going to build it again?"

He shook his head. "No way."

Standing next to her, Zachary shifted his weight, and she rested her hand on top of his head. "We can't just *quit*. We have to start over," Emily said.

Bobby looked at both of them, and then shook his head. "What's the point? It'll probably just get wrecked again, or not even float or something. Why bother?"

Maybe, but maybe not. "It's not really about whether it'll work or not," Emily said. "It's about building it. About, you know, the *dream*."

Bobby kicked a stray piece of wood out of the way. "Emily, you don't get it. We totally wasted our time. All that work, and look what happened."

No, he was missing the point. Yeah, it was disappointing, but that shouldn't be enough to change things. "We *learned* a bunch of stuff," Emily said. "This time, we'll do it even better."

Bobby just shook his head.

Zack was poking his nose into a pile of debris they hadn't examined yet, and Emily went over to see what he had found.

"Hey, look!" she said, and lifted up Bobby's grandfather's old wooden tool chest. "Is it okay?"

Bobby opened it up and checked the tools inside. "Yeah, actually," he said, sounding surprised. "Seems to be fine." He lifted up a weathered chisel, hefting it in his hand. "I guess he built it to last, huh?"

It sure seemed that way.

Bobby stared at the chisel and then put it back neatly in its place in the toolbox.

"So," Emily said. "Where are we going to start?"

Bobby took a deep breath and let it out. Then, he nodded once and stood up. "The frame," he said. "We should lay out what we think our frame will be."

All right, then. Emily nodded back and then studied the ground, trying to imagine the boat that didn't exist yet.

Bobby pointed at the dirt. "We could put in, like, storage areas this time. You know, under the seats?"

"Sort of like drawers?" Emily asked.

He nodded. "Yeah. Or maybe little doors, with hinges. We could put life jackets and stuff in there."

That would be good. It would give them a lot more space to move around.

Zack trotted over to a pile of new, unused boards and used his teeth to yank at the tarpaulin covering it.

"Good boy," Emily said, and helped him pull it off.

Zack grabbed the end of a board in his mouth, his tail waving gently back and forth. Emily and Bobby carried the other end, and they set it down as the first piece of the new frame. They arranged the board on the ground and stepped back to look at it.

"I think we can probably finish by Christmas," Bobby said.

"But we can aim for Thanksgiving," Emily said.

Bobby nodded. "Yup. We can do that."

All around them, other people were doing versions of the same thing—cleaning up the mess, and then, starting over. It had been a really bad storm, but everyone was okay, and now, they just had to rebuild.

"I think the new boat is going to be *twice* as good as the other one," Emily said.

"You know what? I do, too," Bobby said.

Zack barked happily and galloped back to the pile to tug at another piece of plywood to build their frame.

"Do you mind doing this on your birthday?" Bobby asked.

Emily shook her head, lifting the other end of the board. "Actually, it's exactly what I *want* to be doing."

"If you're sure," Bobby said. "My mother took me to get you a new sketch pad and all, but I feel like I should give you something even better."

"Okay. Can we name the boat after Zack?" Emily asked.

Bobby laughed. "You bet. How about the S.S. *Zachary*?"

Yes, that was the perfect name.

They grinned at each other, and helped Zack carry the board to the spot on the ground where the new frame was going to be.

"The S.S. *Zachary* is going to be a really great boat," Bobby said. "I just know it."

Emily nodded. As far as she was concerned, it was going to be the best boat ever!

THE DOG WHISPERER
WILL RETURN

Follow Emily and Zack
on their next adventure in

Dog Whisperer: The Ghost

Available from Square Fish in Fall 2012